CAVE

Bitter unrest among the tribes of the Thamaung Valley in modern Burma threatens a United Nations hydroelectric scheme. Talos Cord, classified as a 'peacemaker' by the UN, arrives to act as arbitrator in the strike of native labourers working on the dam site. There is an undercurrent among the tribesmen that Talos cannot fathom, something mysterious that he senses but cannot identify. He follows a trail that eventually leads him to a deathtrap in a network of caverns and to a grim solution to the mystery.

Books by Bill Knox in the Linford Mystery Library:

SANCTUARY ISLE
LITTLE DROPS OF BLOOD
THE SCAVENGERS
THE MAN IN THE BOTTLE
BLACKLIGHT
JUSTICE ON THE ROCKS
DIE FOR BIG BETSY
DEATH CALLS THE SHOTS
BLUEBACK
WITCHROCK
LIVE BAIT
DRAW BATONS!
PILOT ERROR
THE TALLYMAN
LAKE OF FURY
AN INCIDENT IN ICELAND
PLACE OF MISTS
SALVAGE JOB
A PAY-OFF IN SWITZERLAND
ISLE OF DRAGONS
NEST OF VULTURES
DRUM OF POWER
A PROBLEM IN PRAGUE

BILL KNOX

CAVE OF BATS

Complete and Unabridged

LINFORD
Leicester

First published in the
United States of America
under the name of Robert MacLeod

First Linford Edition
published 1998

British Library CIP Data

Knox, Bill, *1928*–
Cave of bats.—Large print ed.—
Linford mystery library
1. Detective and mystery stories
2. Large type books
I. Title II. MacLeod, Robert *1928*—
823.9′14 [F]

ISBN 0–7089–5350–6

Published by
F. A. Thorpe (Publishing) Ltd.
Anstey, Leicestershire

Set by Words & Graphics Ltd.
Anstey, Leicestershire
Printed and bound in Great Britain by
T. J. International Ltd., Padstow, Cornwall

This book is printed on acid-free paper

For Allan

1

Talos Cord drove down into the Thamaung valley with his foot resting lightly on the accelerator, a snatch of half-forgotten song running through his mind and a fat, yellow-leafed Burmese cheroot glowing happily between his teeth. He was in no desperate hurry; the purr of the pick-up truck's engine matched his mood, and the rich greenery which cloaked each side of the rough, bumping track held the carmine glow of a million blossoming cherry buds.

A small, fat, dapple-coated deer burst from the shadowed woodland on his left and fled across the track into the thick bush beyond. Cord grinned, a lopsided smile which creased across his young, strong-nosed face to halt at the barrier of the old hairline scar running in a curve across his left cheek. February in the highlands of North Burma, a time of warm days and cool evenings, was a month when the world seemed relatively good.

Even the rich red road dust, which for miles now had filmed the small Renault truck's windshield and had all but obliterated the United Nations badge painted bold and white on its doors couldn't change his mood. The job waiting had its problems, but none of these should be impossible to solve.

A fraction of pressure on the accelerator eased the pick-up over a last short incline, then Cord let the Renault coast to a standstill. Below, the rest of his road ran like a brown slash of winding ribbon through the dark green forest and scrub. Beyond, spanning the narrow neck of a widening valley, the squat concrete wall of a dam shimmered in the sunlight.

Three hundred yards across in its buttressed width, the dam was about sixty feet high at the center. But size was less significant than the achievement it represented in the midst of such isolation. And it was still empty of water — apart from the narrow, shallow river which ambled toward it from the upper valley and passed through an opened sluice gate to continue its course into the forest-clad hills.

Cord climbed out of the pick-up's cab, stopped near the hood, and treated himself to the luxury of an animal-like stretch. He knocked a full inch of ash from the cheroot, then returned it to his wide humorous-lipped mouth, and glanced around. He was a compact man, just over medium height, slim and muscular beneath the travel-creased lines of his khaki twill slacks. A lightweight fawn jacket topped his faded blue shirt. He was clean-shaven, with black hair cut short, and the same sunlight which made him narrow his eyes also picked up the scar on his weather-bronzed face, using its line to highlight rather than mar his features.

A cluster of toy-like buildings, marked as Frajon village on the map and lying just below the dam, showed his destination. Above and beyond he saw the valley widen out into vast tree-fringed grassland, with here and there the contrast of brown rectangles of cultivated land.

Harsh hills surrounded the valley's plain, rising sharply to the north, stacking and bulking into the snow-capped peaks of distant mountains.

Nearer to him, at the valley's neck, the right shoulder of the dam rested on a fairly modest hill. In contrast, the left shoulder met the flank of a rapidly rising slope, which was the start of a massive crag of rock reaching up toward the clouds. Another, smaller sprinkling of huts and buildings sat high on the slope, perched beside great spoil-heaps of quarried rubble. From there, a path ran down to the dam's waiting basin. The water would come that way in time, tunneled through from the other side of the ridge.

Cord had seen enough. He tossed away the cheroot stub, swung himself back into the Renault's cab, and set the little vehicle rolling. Fifteen minutes later he reached the outskirts of the village.

Frajon was a place divided into two separate worlds, part Burmese-style log-and-thatch houses, part modern single-story sectional blocks set on brick foundations. And it was quiet, unnaturally quiet for mid-afternoon in what should have been the bustling headquarters of the U.N.-sponsored Thamaung Valley project. A few children played around the thatch houses and a half-asleep dog stirred lazily to bark as the pick-up went past. Plenty of eyes might be watching him, but Cord saw only one adult, a woman who promptly vanished again into the shade of her doorway.

On the far side of the village, where the project buildings began, there was only a degree of difference. A handful of men, thin, dark-skinned southerners — not the stocky, light-complexioned hill dwellers — were languidly loading cement a bag at a time onto a wide-tired truck. There was little other activity as Talos drove on. The Thamaung project's main labor force was on strike, had been for almost a week, and the project appeared close to a complete standstill.

Cord steered the Renault toward one of the largest of the buildings and pulled in beside a line of parked vehicles.

'Hey, a moment!' The voice, with a

loud, rasping Italian accent, hailed Talos as he stepped down from the pick-up. A fat, bearded figure in stained overalls — an old blue beret crammed firmly on his head — waved an arm and hurried toward him.

'Signor Cord? Prinetti, general foreman. Signor Lewis told me to watch for you to arrive.'

'Good.' Cord jerked his head in the direction of the village. 'Any change over there?'

'*Niente*,' said Prinetti with a brief scowl. 'They still refuse to work. You know these hill people?'

'A little.' A very little. But there were other reasons for his arrival. U.N. Field Reconnaisance, the nearest thing in existence to an international security service, didn't send any of its few men on jobs like the ironing out of backwood labor disputes, however embarrassing the dispute concerned might be.

'Huh.' The Italian swept him with a look. 'These are Pulos. They'll tell you they came here originally from the north. Strong as mules — and as stubborn.

Peccato! When they work, they earn every kyat note they're paid.'

'So I've heard.' Cord nodded.

'Well,' the other man sighed, 'I take you to Signor Lewis, I guess.'

Cord followed him, brushing the worst of the travel dust from his clothes as they entered the building and went along a short corridor.

Prinetti pushed his way through the glass swinging door at the far end, and a pert, well-rounded Anglo-Burmese girl rose from her typewriter and greeted them with a smile. Her native-style rainbow silk blouse, worn over a straight-cut linen skirt, made a splash of vivid color against the dull efficiency of the room.

'Signor Cord,' said Prinetti briefly. 'Can we go in, Lona?'

The girl smiled again, her dark eyes sweeping over Cord with quick, appreciative interest. She nodded. 'They are waiting.'

Prinetti grunted, tapped briefly on the other door in the room, then opened it and ushered Cord in ahead of him.

There were three people in the office

beyond. The nearest was a dark, chunkily-built Burmese in tight-fitting army battle dress. Beside him was a tall, thin, almost bald European of about sixty. He wore crumpled fawn drill slacks and shift, a plain black tie was knotted loosely at his neck, and his lined, long-jawed face showed a faint stubble of beard. The third person was a girl. She stood farther back, twin spots of red flushing her cheeks.

'Talos Cord?' The older man crossed the uncarpeted floor, extending his hand in welcome, the soft round vowels of England's southwest almost submerged beneath a civil service precision. 'I'm Henry Lewis. It's a pleasure to meet you.' The Thamaung Valley project chief had a grip which was damp but firm. 'This is Captain Sen Paya, who is local military commander' — the heavy faced soldier gave a slow, cautious nod at the introduction — 'and Marian Frey, our resettlement officer.'

'Which means I'm particularly glad to see you,' she said thankfully. 'It's about time we had some help.'

The soldier snorted at her words, but

for the moment Cord was otherwise interested. Marian Frey was a brunette, small and slim-waisted, dressed like Lewis in slacks and shirt. But her outfit was in tailored linen and served against its will to accentuate the neat, youthfully firm figure beneath. A blue silk scarf was knotted at her throat, and her face was heart-shaped, with cool gray eyes and a mouth which still held a trace of tight anger left over from whatever he'd interrupted. The lips bore a faint touch of almost neutral lipstick and her hair was caught back in what, on another woman, might have seemed an almost juvenile ponytail. But on her it seemed both right and practical.

'Any trouble on the way, Cord?' queried Lewis.

'None,' he assured them. 'I left Myitkyina this morning.'

Before that there had been a jet flight from Singapore to Rangoon, then another plane north; but plane flights were cocoon-living, not travel.

'That's good. The road journey can be a trial at times.' Lewis glanced toward

Prinetti, standing patiently at the door. 'You've made arrangements as I asked?'

'*Si*. They are there.' The foreman scratched his beard. 'You want me along?'

Lewis nodded. 'Yes. Don't be too far away. And have one of the men take Mr. Cord's gear over to the guest hut.'

Prinetti gave a grunt of acknowledgment and went out, closing the door hard behind him.

Lewis gave a rueful grimace. 'An excellent man, our Prinetti. But not in the best of humor right now. Come to that, I suppose, none of us are.' He gestured toward the nearest chair. 'You must be feeling tired.'

'I'd rather stand, for the novelty of it.'

Hands in his pockets, Cord took a frankly curious glance around. Henry Lewis' office was very much a work place. Graph charts and survey maps were taped to the walls alongside a series of aerial photo blow-ups. The project chief's desk was of plain, unvarnished wood; the filing cabinets of sturdy, utilitarian metal; and the big drawing board in the far corner sat on an obviously home-made bench.

'Mr. Cord,' Captain Paya broke his silence, a hint of reluctance in his manner. 'I would be glad if you would tell me just why you are here.' He pursed his lips. 'The Thamaung *ching* — this valley — is under my administration. But I have no instructions from my headquarters at Myitkyina concerning you — or your authority. All I have been told is that another Englishman would be arriving and that he would be some form of peacemaker.'

Cord tried to thaw the man with a friendly grin. 'I've no direct authority from your government, Captain. But they know I'm here. This is a U.N. technical aid project, most of the money comes from UNESCO, and we want to sort out whatever it has run up against.'

'And this name of 'peacemaker'?' The soldier was still warily suspicious.

'Just a phrase.' Cord dismissed it with an easy chuckle, perching himself on the edge of Lewis' desk. 'I'm with what's called Field Reconnaissance. Problems are our specialty — you could say I'm a type of mobile advisor.'

'I see.' The helping of half-truths seemed to satisfy the soldier, and he relaxed a little. 'Then perhaps you can 'advise' your people on this. I have suggested that the time may be ripe for a show of strength.'

'Army-style strength?' Cord glanced toward the girl, saw her mouth tightening, and guessed this was where he'd come in. 'What's the security set-up at the moment?'

'A sergeant and six men forming a police post,' said Marian Frey shortly. 'Captain Paya wants to bring in more men.'

'But you're against it?'

She gave a crisp, hopeful nod.

'Ordinarily I would be too.' Lewis frowned, fingers plucking absently at his loosened tie. 'But this time I'm not sure; there's a reason why I think it might help.'

'And it's almost as mad as the reason why these people have stopped work,' protested the girl. 'We ask them to help us flood their valley with the promise they'll get compensation, new homes, better land. Suddenly they decide that all we've been promising is a lie — well, that's bad enough. But it'll be ten times worse if they get the idea we're trying to force them back to work at the point of a rifle.'

'We know who told them we were lying,' said Lewis softly. 'That's what makes the difference.'

'A dangerous difference,' snorted Captain Paya, 'a renegade, a branded rebel named Nam Ree, hiding up in the hills with more of his kind.'

'A rebel,' agreed Lewis. 'But he's a Pulo; this valley is his home; and he's got plenty of friends. Until now we've had no trouble from him, but if he wanted to back this labor strike with more than words . . . '

'Then a sergeant and six men wouldn't stop him,' Cord agreed, the humor gone from his manner. 'Any idea why he started this trouble?'

'None.' Lewis gave a heavy sigh. 'I wondered — perhaps if we took a deputation of villagers to the resettlement area it would help.'

'Take them a hundred miles so they can see for themselves nothing is ready?' Cord broke the news with gentle cynicism, knowing it would cause consternation. 'It happens Nam Ree is fairly close to the truth. The land's there, yes. But that's about all. There's not a house complete, hardly anything else more than half-built.' He saw Lewis' blank disbelief. 'When did you plan to move the first party to the resettlement zone?'

'In — in about two weeks' time!' Lewis swallowed back his confusion.

'Miss Frey, when did you last have any real contact with the resettlement team?'

The gray eyes still showed shock. 'Not for two or three weeks. I'd wondered. I'd written them about several things.'

'Damn it, why weren't we told?' Lewis' thin face showed an angry flush; his voice was like grating gravel.

'They were ordered to keep quiet about it,' said Cord bluntly. 'There was a good enough reason at the beginning

— Project Planning headquarters didn't want rumors spreading — they hoped the program could catch up on itself, and stage one was just a strike over pay and conditions among the imported work force.'

'Even so,' Lewis gave a growl.

'That was stage one.' Cord cut him short. 'The men went back, and then there was a wave of arson and thievery. The program began to collapse, and last week most of the labor force suddenly put down their tools, drew their pay, and walked off. There are all the signs that somebody set out to wreck the scheme — and succeeded.'

'If we tell the Pulos this, then anything might happen.' Lewis bit his lip. 'Hell, man, what can we do?'

Captain Paya had his own solution. 'I can get the first of my men here within a couple of hours,' he volunteered enthusiastically.

Cord shook his head. 'No, not yet. Miss Frey's right. We don't want army intervention in any form until we've run out of other ideas.' He saw relief on the girl's face, but Captain Paya's reaction was immediate protest.

'The responsibility . . . '

'The responsibility will be mine.' Cord's young, dark-tanned face grew suddenly hard. 'This is your district, Captain. But what would they say back in Myitkyina if you took on too much responsibility too soon and turned a strike into a rebellion? How would you stand if your general got a U.N. observer's report saying the whole thing was sparked off because you acted against advice?'

'You have another way?' Paya's dignity was ruffled, but the implied threat had had its effect.

'Maybe.' Cord was noncommittal.

Paya shrugged. 'All right, Mr. Cord. But my men will be on stand-by.' He tapped the leather holster at his waist. 'If it comes to this, I will like it no more than you. But if we arrive too late, I will have a report of my own to make.'

The soldier snatched up his service beret from Lewis' desk, gave a brief nod, and marched out, the door slamming behind him. A moment later they heard a jeep engine bark to life outside, and then the squeal of tires as it drove off.

'Well now,' Lewis took a deep breath and forced a feeble smile, 'I could use a cup of coffee. And a chance to think.'

'I'll get it.' Marian Frey went over to the metal pot steaming gently on a small hotplate, found some paper cups, and began pouring. She smiled as she gave the first cup to Cord, then put one down beside Lewis, and took the other for herself.

'Why couldn't they have warned us about the resettlement situation?' Lewis strode restlessly across the floor, then turned, his thin fists tightly clenched. 'Why only now? For months we've been telling the people here that everything would be fine!'

'It should have been.' Cord gave a sympathetic shrug. 'They held on to their hopes, held on a little too long. But what decided things was your report from here that the Pulos had stopped work, stopped the day after the labor force at the resettlement zone walked out. Nam Ree's grapevine may be good, but that sort of timing was too much to swallow.'

'It doesn't make sense.' Marian Frey sat down in the chair opposite him, and her gray eyes held his own. 'What reason could there be? Why would he do it?'

'That's what I'm supposed to find out.' Cord tasted the coffee. It was strong and sweet, as he liked it. 'Lewis, if you got your labor force back to work tomorrow, how long would it take to finish the job?'

'Ten, say twelve days at the most. You know the plan?'

'In outline, yes. In detail, no.' Cord made it an invitation, and the project chief seemed happy at the chance to escape from his more immediate troubles.

'This is in fairly small scale, but it'll do.' Lewis seized a rolled-up map and spread it over the desk. A long forefinger stabbed down at the paper. 'Here's the Thamaung district about eight hundred square miles of territory, mostly hills and mountains except for two sections. One is the Thamaung Valley, where we are. It's over twenty miles long and goes to almost five miles wide. The other is this low, flat area to the west, the Sihrong. It's half-a-dozen times as big as the Thamaung Valley, but mainly swamp and marsh.'

Cord looked at the heavily shaded contours and nodded. 'Sounds not much use to anyone.'

'The Sihrong?' Marian Frey spoke with confident conviction. 'Not yet, but it will be. The soil is rich; it could be reclaimed.'

'And that's one of the reasons we're here.' Lewis picked up a pencil and began to trace his way across the map. 'Here's the Thamaung Valley with the Thamaung River coming down from the north. It's a small river, but it has a clear route through the hills to the south. Now here's our dam. The tunnel site begins — well, you saw that for yourself coming in. That mass of rock opposite us is the start of the Dolpha Ridge, running between seven and ten thousand feet. Just the other side of the Dolpha and about a thousand feet above our level is Lake Mawtayn. It's big, deep, and snow-fed every spring from the mountains up north.

'But what happens to it?' Lewis paused dramatically. 'It overflows on low ground to the west, away from here. Goes wandering for a couple of miles, then floods out into the Sihrong swampland. A complete waste. So,' the pencil jabbed, 'we've built our dam. We've tunneled through the Dolpha Ridge. Once we get to the right spot, under Lake Mawtayn, we'll blast out the last few feet of rock with explosives. It'll be like pushing the plug out of a bathtub, and we'll get the water here.'

'Whereupon the Thamaung Valley floods,' said Cord dryly.

'It floods,' agreed Lewis. 'We make a new lake here, about twenty miles long. But we dry out the Sihrong and reclaim six times as much land as we lose, six times as much *good* land. Even that's just the start. We generate hydroelectric power from the Thamaung dam. We run it by cable to where we want it. Electric power, Cord, something unknown around here. Do you know the nearest thing to an industry within eighty miles as things stand? One played-out ruby mine half-way up the valley.' An almost fanatical gleam lit his eyes. 'Well, things are going to be different, very different.'

'What about people?' asked Cord. 'How many will have to move out?'

Lewis glanced at Marian Frey. She frowned. 'We estimate about two thousand from about a dozen villages in the lower valley. There's roughly another four thousand living in the Thamaung district, but their homes are either in the hills or in the *kou*, the higher valley ground well above planned water level.'

'Moving people is unfortunate.' A brief shadow crossed Lewis' face. 'But think of the dividend in human terms, in work, in prosperity for the area. The forest can start producing timber from local sawmills, powered sawmills. We can start pump-irrigation schemes lower down the river, maybe even prime some light industries into operation. It's been done in other places, and it can be done here — once there's power on tap.'

'Which means once the tunnel goes through and the Pulos have moved.' Cord drank the last of his coffee, squashed the paper cup, and tossed it into a wastebasket. 'Lewis, you're working less than forty miles from the border with Red China. Ever thought they might have an interest in all this?'

'You mean, could they be trying to stop it?' The project chief blinked incredulously. 'Good heavens, man, don't tell me you came here just to wave that sort of nonsense around. There's nothing, absolutely nothing here but hills and rocks.'

'People said that about Tibet,' Cord reminded him softly.

'Different circumstances.' Lewis snapped the words. 'Marian, don't you agree?'

She seemed bitterly amused. 'I hoped for something better from you, Mr. Cord, especially after the way you were against Captain Paya moving in troops. All right, someone is trying to stop us. But even if this someone is Nam Ree, he's no Communist. Even Captain Paya would agree on that.'

'I only asked.' Cord let the matter drop. 'Well, the obvious thing I've got to do next is have a talk with some of the local headmen. Can you fix it?'

'That's already arranged,' said Lewis with pleased satisfaction. 'I had Prinetti tell them we'd want a meeting. When do you want to see them?'

'Anything wrong with right now?'

'Absolutely nothing.' The project chief rolled up the map and tossed it back on his desk. 'Like to come along, Marian?'

She shook her head. 'I'll stay. I'm not sure I could face them after all the promises I've made.' Her voice stopped the two men as they reached the door. 'Mr. Cord, what do you plan to tell them?'

Cord rubbed his chin. 'The only thing that may do some good — the truth. But don't let it worry you.' He chuckled. 'The unorthodox has a habit of winning a trick.'

* * *

The same unreal quiet as before reigned outside the headquarters block. Lewis led the way, identifying the various buildings as they crossed the compound — the radio hut with its tall slim aerial, the medical dispensary, the transport section, living quarters, the brick shed which housed their temporary diesel generator, the police post — all the other units which made up the Thamaung base.

Over at the main store shed the same handful of Burmese still lounged in the open, though the cement truck they'd been loading had gone. They made only a half-hearted attempt to appear busy as the two U.N. men passed.

'Can't blame them,' said Lewis. 'Anyway, we've just about run out of odd jobs to keep them going.'

'Couldn't you use them at the tunnel?'

'And try finishing it off without the Pulos?' Lewis shook his head. 'Not a chance. There's still a couple of hundred feet of granite rock between us and the lake.'

'Even mustering every man you could find?'

'Still not a chance. I've a staff of fourteen here, mostly Europeans, nearly all specialist technicians. We brought about thirty Burmese from the south with us, but they're truck drivers, clerks, cooks, that sort of thing. This is a brain-and-muscle operation; the Pulos are our muscles, and we need them, even with modern equipment.'

'You've tried it?'

'We did, for one day. The work nearly killed half of us. Ask Prinetti.' Lewis slowed his stride, looking around. 'There he is, coming down the hill. I told him to be ready.'

The Italian foreman met them as they reached the boundary of the old village, his face red with anger. 'I been up at the tunnel,' he exploded, ignoring all preliminaries. 'You know what? I find six, seven Pulos up there making sure nobody goes through to start work!'

'Pickets . . . ' Lewis shook his head and sighed. 'That's a new one from them. Did they let you pass?'

'Me? You think I ask them if I can go see my own tunnel?' Prinetti rumbled into his beard at the idea. 'I went in. She's okay inside.'

He fell into step with them and they

entered the village. At closer inspection it consisted of about forty wooden huts, each standing a few feet off the ground on broad wooden stilts, and each with its small, neat garden beneath. Smoke trailed from several of the thatched roofs, but even the children Cord had seen when he'd driven through earlier had now vanished.

'Here we are.' Lewis signed them to a halt outside one of the huts, distinguished from its neighbors by having a large, beaten-flat kerosene can hanging outside its tiny porch as an alarm gong. 'The man who'll do their talking is Myi Teri. He's a decent enough old devil, but he doesn't like being rushed. Whatever you've got in mind, Cord, remember that.'

They climbed the half-dozen rough teakwood steps to the porch and a somber-faced young Pulo hillman appeared in the doorway, beckoning them on. Lewis nodded, and they went in.

At a rough count there were a score of men in the gloom of the one big room. It was hard to be accurate. Smoke from the

wood-chip fire burning on a ru
plate in the center of the floor s
Cord's eyes as he had his first
the men of Frajon village.

The Pulos — squat, stocky, muscular little men, their faces hard and suspicious in the glowing firelight — sat on mats and stools at the far end of the hut. Most wore the inevitable workday shirt and shorts and a loose cotton turban. A few of the younger men were stripped to the waist and bareheaded. One or two wrinkle-faced elders had antiquated army overcoats draped on their shoulders.

Only one man, in the front center of the group, rose to his feet to greet them. He was gray-haired and broken gaps showed in his teeth when he parted his lips in a token greeting. But his bearing was erect and proud, his eyes bright and steady, and he had prepared himself with some attention for his role. In contrast to the others, his headgear was of black silk. His blue woven jacket was buttoned to the throat and embroidered in silver, and his spotless, skirt-like *loongyi* was a candy-striped red and yellow. In both ess and bearing he was in the traditional pattern of the hill peoples' leaders.

'Myi Teri,' said Prinetti in a soft undertone. 'An old man, but no fool. What he decides, the rest will do.'

Cord gave a faint nod and stood quietly, conscious of the gallery's scrutiny, while Henry Lewis went through the formalities of introducing him. He spoke in English, and included a hopeful phrase or two about peaceful understanding. A low mutter of voices from his audience showed that the Pulos had their own translators.

Myi Teri gave a gravely polite nod as the project chief finished. 'Your friend will find we are always ready to listen, Mr. Lewis.' He looked down at the fire, silent for a moment, then raised his head. 'But things are as we have told you; we will not work in the tunnel. We have had enough of false promises.'

The background mutter rose, then subsided again as Lewis spread his hands appealingly. 'But doesn't the good this tunnel will bring, the prosperity that comes with it, mean anything to you?'

'The good is for others, not for the Pulos. Or,' Myi Teri's bright dark eyes focused on Cord, 'does your friend have something new to tell us, something better than the old story that we know was a lie?' Behind him, a toothless old straggle-beard spat a comment of his own, and got a growl of support from the others.

Cord took his time, letting the simmer of agreement go its course. One or two of the Pulos hadn't joined in the hubbub. The nearest was taller than the others but equally broad-boned. His dress was identical to theirs, his face round and button-nosed, high cheek-boned, his chin resting on the palm of one hand. What made him stand out, however, was the glint of something close to amusement which wrinkled the skin around his deep-set eyes when a neighbor leaned forward, nudged him, and appeared to mutter a question. A brief head-shake was the only sign of reply.

Myi Teri raised his hand and the gathering fell silent. 'There is another matter. Our people in the upper *ching*, whose homes would be above the new lake, were promised that when the water came it would not cover the entrance to their holy *ku*. But some of your people were there two days ago. Why?' He seemed slightly embarrassed as he added, 'This concerns the old ones, whose time is short. But what concerns them must concern us all.'

Puzzled, Cord hesitated and glanced questioningly toward Lewis.

'This *ku* is one of the caves up the valley, beyond Ronul,' muttered the project chief. 'There's an altar inside to one of the old mountain gods. Some of the Pulos are still animists; we've had to step carefully.'

'Will it be flooded?'

'No. All that happened was that three of our men went sight-seeing. I'm dealing with them.'

'Right.' Cord nodded and took a step forward into the smoke-filtered light. 'You ask for answers,' he told the villagers. 'That's why I have been sent here.' He watched them as he went on in the same neutral, factual voice. 'This man in the hills, Nam Ree, has said there are no new homes waiting for you. Well, what he says is true.'

'True . . . ' Myi Teri's lips twisted back in angry amazement. 'You admit the lies?'

Behind him there was a quick mutter of translation, then an ominous, absolute silence. The button-nosed man had leaned forward a little. Near him, a big burly Pulo, a heavy gold ring through his left earlobe, rose ponderously to his feet.

'There were no lies. The people here told you what they thought to be truth. And there is land, good land and ready for planting.' Cord grasped the advantage while he could. 'New homes were being built — new homes and many other things. It was a job for many men. But these men have stopped work and have gone away. They became greedy for money and listened to others who wanted only trouble. Blame these troublemakers that your new homes are not ready. As for your holy *ku*' — Cord shook his head — 'the men who went there wanted only to visit it. The water will not reach it.'

The burly Pulo with the earring gave a grunt. '*To-pan* what good is all this to us?' he boomed in slow, halting English. 'You have no place for us to go, yet if the water comes to the valley there will be no place for us here. Have we to stay and drown? Or have we to take our families into the mountains and grow rice on rocks?'

He stood there, scowling, while the muttering grew and more of the Pulos rose to their feet. The firelight glinted on a knife blade, then the quiet button-nosed man's hand left his chin, an excited young hillman received a quick cuff across the mouth, and the knife vanished again.

'Can you answer that, Mr. Cord?' Myi Teri's face was grim. 'Do you expect us to bring ruin on our families?'

'No.' Cord gambled on the headman's pride. 'But I want you to help yourselves. This new land is waiting to the south. Your villages have the men who can finish the tunnel. Do they also have men who will go to the new land and help us to build homes for themselves

and for those who work in the tunnel?'
He gauged the effect of his words from the indecision on the headman's face, and gave the Pulos' pride a final twist. 'You say we have failed in our promises. We will fail — unless your people have the strength in their hands and minds to help make our promises come true. Or will you huddle in the valley like children until other men can be found to do the work for you?'

Myi Teri was uncertain, caught off balance. 'If this is meant . . . '

'It is meant. And all who help will be well paid.'

The headman frowned. 'Even so, I can only speak for some of our people. Not all the *ching* villages have men here.'

'Then call them, talk about it, and give your answer tomorrow.'

Cord judged he'd achieved maximum effect. The thing to do now was to get out and let the Pulos argue. He gave a quick, formal gesture of farewell, then swept Lewis and Prinetti along with him toward the hut door.

The rumble of raised voices had begun

before they reached the path outside, but the three men kept going without glancing back.

'You've found a way out, if they agree.' Lewis slowed his pace a little as they walked toward the project compound. He drew one thin hand across a brow damp with nervous perspiration. 'But — but if they say yes, do you have the authority to arrange all this?'

'Arranging it will be up to you and Marian Frey, but I'll make sure you have the authorization by tonight,' Cord assured him. He glanced at Prinetti, who was walking beside them, hands deep in his pockets. 'Well, what do you think they'll do?'

'Maybe they say yes, maybe no.' The Italian scraped at his beard. 'These Pulos are independent as hell. That last moment, when you tell them maybe they haven't the guts to do it themselves . . .' He guffawed at the recollection. 'We were lucky to walk out of there in one piece. You saw the one with the knife, earlier?'

'Excitement, pure excitement,' said

Lewis swiftly. 'Nothing would have happened.'

'Ha!' Prinetti rolled his eyes skyward. 'Signor Cord, you saw the man who stopped him?'

'Button-nose?' Cord showed his interest at the same time as he heard Lewis give a faint groan of despair. 'Who was he?'

'The fellow who causes all this trouble in the first place. Nam Ree,' said Prinetti explosively. 'Well, you gave him something to think about, eh?'

'Nam Ree . . . ' Cord swung around on Lewis. 'You knew this?' He read the confirmation in the man's flushed face, and swore softly. 'Why didn't you tell me he was there? He's the one man I really want to talk with!'

'Because — because I didn't want trouble.' Lewis looked away for a moment, biting on his lip. When he turned again there was something close to an appeal in his eyes. 'Cord, all I'm interested in is getting this mess sorted out. We know Nam Ree comes regularly into the village, and that he sits in on most of the Pulo councils.' His voice slowed, emphasizing. 'But we just pretend he's not there. Can you understand?'

Talos Cord shrugged his bewilderment. 'Does Captain Paya know this happens?'

Lewis shook his head. 'Paya once showed us a photograph of the man and asked us to keep our eyes open. But we've had no quarrel with Nam Ree, even if he is a rebel, no quarrel until now anyway. If we told the Burmese authorities and Nam Ree was captured as a result, the Pulos would have nothing more to do with us.'

Prinetti gave an awkward rumble, conscious of starting the trouble between them. 'Look at it this way, Signor Cord. Suppose we had told you in the hut that Nam Ree was there, maybe you'd have tried to talk with him. That way . . . ' He spat expressively. 'They don't trust strangers. Maybe none of us would have gotten out of that hut. Sure, it sounds crazy. We pretend we don' know he's there. The Pulos — well — maybe they know we pretend. But it works.'

Cord took a last look back at the headman's hut. All his instincts told him to go back and try to make direct contact with the Pulo rebel. But there was a strange yet understandable logic behind the project men's attitude. If he were to meet Nam Ree, then it would have to be another way. The almost comic madness of the situation got the upper hand in his mind. He gave a rueful grin, and his two companions seemed relieved as he relaxed into the easy-going mood they'd previously known.

'Well, it's too late to do anything about it now,' he declared. 'Let's leave it. Anyway, I could use a wash, a drink, and some food. It's been a long time since breakfast.'

Lewis brightened visibly. 'Well, we eat at eight. But if you'll settle for whatever the kitchen can put together until then . . . '

'That's all I ask,' Cord told him.

They split up at the project compound, Lewis heading for his office, Prinetti guiding Cord toward the camp guest hut. It was a small, chalet-like building set a little way back from the rest of the project camp. Sparsely but adequately furnished, it had a window which gave a view across the dam site to the high brooding mass of the Dolpha Ridge and the tunnel location. Once inside, Prinetti fussed around, making sure that all was in order, even checking the washbasin and its piped water supply.

'Everything's fine,' Cord assured him.

'*Buono*.' The foreman beamed. 'I tell the kitchen to get that meal for you, then I think I go and tell my wife I'm still in one piece. She worries.'

'Your wife is here?' Cord turned from the window mildly surprised.

'Sure,' nodded Prinetti. 'My Anna was camp nurse in a scheme in Iraq. I meet her there. Then I offer her a better job, eh? We got a boy now, nearly two years old. Victor, same name as me.' He opened the door. 'Remember, anything you want, you just let me know. Okay?'

Left alone, Cord gave way to weariness. He took off his jacket, loosened his tie and collar, and flopped on his back on the bed beside his single lightweight suitcase.

The Pulos would say yes. He felt sure

enough to bet on it. Their pride had been stung and, whatever Nam Ree's influence, they'd been left with no real alternative. He found his cigarettes, lit one, and blew a lazy cloud of smoke toward the low ceiling. Nam Ree — sitting there among the Pulo leaders. That was a situation he hadn't expected.

His chuckle changed to a grimace as another name crossed his mind — Andrew Beck, chief of Field Reconnaisance back at U.N. headquarters in New York. It was Beck who had ordered him to the Thamaung Valley, Beck with his fat untidy body, his three telephones and his world map, his nose for rumor and pending trouble, his matter-of-fact way of moving a man like a rogue knight on the international chessboard then letting events decide what followed.

'Peacemakers . . . ' That had been Lewis' description of the Field Reconnaisance section. Well, it was reasonable. Their specialty was finding out what was going on when trouble began simmering, then advising the top brass on the best way to stop the situation from boiling over.

Cord rolled over on his side, stubbed out the cigarette in an ash tray placed beside the bed, and settled back. The last two jobs for Beck had been in the soft category. London — for a reason which would have surprised at least one member of Her Majesty's government. Then Singapore — though the task there had turned out to be a pure fiasco of misunderstanding. But what came next on this one?

The next stage was plain. He had to find out more about Nam Ree. It seemed barely possible that the Pulo rebel would have acted against his own people by engineering the collapse of the resettlement program. Yet how had he known so quickly that the resettlement workers had walked out on the job? And behind Nam Ree loomed a larger shadow. The gentle questions Cord had put to Lewis about the Thamaung project's proximity to the Chinese border had been neither idle nor speculative. The cabled, coded briefing sent by Andrew Beck had been short and precise — 'Analysis of reports from external sources suggests Chinese interest in Thamaung dispute. Wider implications likely, details indefinite. Investigate.'

North Burma was always a potential tinderbox, wedged as it was between India and Communist China. The Chinese-Indian border dispute still remained as a lurking, smoldering potential. Even though Burma might want to stay peacefully neutral, her position was crucially awkward — and not just to the north. To the east lay open warfare in South Viet Nam. To the south was Malaysia, with Red terrorists still hiding in her jungles and Indonesia making newer, angry noises on her doorstep.

If the Chinese planned fresh trouble, trouble in North Burma, it could be the start to an explosion of violence almost anywhere in southeast Asia.

He shrugged. At least Beck had offered a word or two about Henry Lewis — 'English nationality, hydroelectric engineering specialist, ten years U.N. service, A.1. reliable.' Lewis was one of the new breed of international civil servants. When they signed on, they swore to exercise all 'loyalty, discretion, and conscience' to their U.N. role. A polite way of saying they had to forget their previous national ties whatever the situation that arose.

Lewis was a bit of an old woman. But Cord liked him, liked him for a man single-minded enough not to give a hoot about anything except the job he'd been given to do. But that, as Cord had already found out, didn't make Lewis the easiest of people to deal with.

Cord yawned, stretched, then made a lazy cat-roll which took him off the bed and onto his feet. He had washed and was ready when a gentle tap fell on the door. A young Burmese wearing a white mess jacket entered, balancing a laden, cloth-covered tray in one hand. The youngster deftly set the tray down on the table and placed a chair in front of it. He whisked off the cloth, gave a bobbing bow, and left as silently as he had come.

The meal was a succulently substantial curry of chicken and pork with fish and fruit, all bedded on hillocking rice. Thin, hot, fresh chupatties were in a covered dish to one side, flanked by a bottle of English lager which was topped by an upturned glass.

Cord ate with relish, washed the meal down with the beer, and finished off by lighting the last of the handful of eight-inch cheroots he'd bought back at Myitkyina.

He went back to the suitcase, opened it, located paper and a pencil, and spent half the cheroot's length coding out a fifty-word cable. It was addressed to the U.N. mission at Rangoon, but the opening prefix letters would insure it priority handling from there on.

The walk down to the radio hut held one item of hopeful interest. He saw that the Pulo village was coming back to life. Men and women were moving around between the houses; children swarmed at their games; and even some of the dogs and poultry, previously conspicuously absent, were now rooting around beneath the stilts of the buildings.

The operator at the radio hut was a slight, red-haired youngster with a broad Scots accent. 'Donaldson's the name, Andy Donaldson.' He cheerfully introduced himself. 'Nice to see a new face around here.'

Cord showed him the coded cable. 'How soon can you send this off?'

'For Rangoon, eh?' The young radioman scratched his fiery mop with one stubby forefinger. 'Well now, that depends on the army signal corps lads at Nanshu, Mr. Cord.' He gestured toward his transmitter key. 'The hills around here play merry hell wi' signals. If they'd give me a remote aerial up on top of the Dolpha everything would be fine. But as it is, I call up the army camp at Nanshu. They patch in a relay and boost my signal to Myitkyina. There's a full-power station there, and it does the rest.'

'How far is it to Nanshu?' asked Cord, glancing around the room with its pasted pin-up pictures and cartoon drawings.

'Twenty miles beyond the valley in a straight line, forty by the mountain road,' said Donaldson. 'And a miserable road it is, too.'

'I found that out for myself.' Cord

watched the radioman note the message's origin and destination into the station log-book. It was only the third entry for the day. 'Business slack at the moment?'

'Here?' Donaldson shook his head. 'Ach, this place can be so quiet it would drive you daft.'

'No other local stations you can call up for a gossip?'

'Well . . . ' Donaldson rubbed his chin and inspected his visitor with greater care. 'There's no other station officially, if you know what I mean. But the army lads at Nanshu say somebody's been using a low-power transmitter in the area.'

'A pirate set?' Cord's interest sharpened. 'Have you heard it operating?'

'That's what the army asked me. They wanted to see if I could give them a radio bearing. But I've only heard it once; and it was just the tail end of a message, too short for me to get a fix.'

'A code message?'

'Aye.' Donaldson dismissed the matter. 'If you ask me, it was a station the other side of the Chinese border. These mountains can play tricks wi' signals, and there's plenty o' military stations workin' over there.' He gave a sniff of pure professional derision. 'They're no' very good at operating either.'

Cord stayed while the youngster made contact with Nanshu and confirmed that the Myitkyina relay was available. Then, as the Morse groups began crackling out, he left Donaldson to his task and began a thoughtful exploration around the camp. A few minutes brought him almost inevitably to the high wall of the dam, and he walked along its base line to the open sluice gates. The slow-moving water of the Thamaung River was gurgling steadily through the flume before spreading back into the bed of its natural, shallow course.

A flimsy wooden bridge, two planks wide, had been laid across the river for foot traffic, leaving vehicles to use a ford set lower down. Cord crossed the swaying planks to the ground on the far side, then followed the dry rutted path which toiled up the rising hillside beyond. He was sweating with exertion by the time he reached the first of the tunnel spoil-heaps lying some four hundred feet up. From there on, for another two hundred feet or so, the spoil-heaps formed an untidy chain, dull dead mounds of excavated material, the more recent easily identified by their almost one hundred per cent content of raw broken granite.

If there had been vegetation around the tunnel site, it had long since been overpowered. Only stubbled grass and a few pathetically broken stumps of shrub showed that nature hadn't completely given up hope of reasserting her role.

Above the spoil-heaps began the vast miscellany of the operation's needs — bulking dumps of cement and sand, huge curved sheets of galvanized steel shutter lining, stocks of the large-bore pipes which would eventually carry the tunnel water down the open hillside to the future lake below. The brick-built valve house which would control the flow seemed near completion and was flanked by a cluster of wooden huts. Over to the far right, isolated from the rest, was a much smaller brick-built bunker with a heavy door. Along its side, painted in foot-high lettering, were the words EXPLOSIVES — KEEP OFF.

For the first time since he'd left the camp, Cord saw he had company. A khaki-clad soldier lounged against the wall of the explosives magazine, a rifle slung over one shoulder. Captain Paya's police detail was still wearily on duty, a token comfort, if nothing else, to the strike-bound camp.

Another minute's walk, following the bright steel of a light rail track, brought Cord to the tunnel mouth. It was concrete lined, about fifteen feet in diameter, the rail track's twin ribbons fading into the gloom which lay within.

A soft whisper of movement around him jerked Cord's eyes from the dark silent tunnel. The nearest less than a dozen feet away, each with a long *dah* knife at his waist suspended from a leather shoulder belt, four of the Pulos stood watching him.

The knives were to be expected. No self-respecting Burmese hillman would have felt properly dressed without his *dah*, that two-foot long, blunt-pointed, and beautifully balanced work tool which was almost an extension of his right arm. Habitually razor-sharp, multi-purpose from slashing a path to digging a hole, the *dah* was a mixture of sword and cleaver — and demanded frightening respect at close quarters.

The Pulos came nearer. Cord waited, saying nothing, while two of them moved to stand between him and the tunnel. Still not a hand had touched the sweat-blackened wood of the *dah* hilts, and the broad faces were impassive. But their meaning was clear. Prinetti might have pushed his way through the tunnel picket by sheer determination. The next to try it might not be so lucky. Cord glanced to his right, but the explosives magazine and its indolent sentry were out of sight behind the bulk of a high stack of waterpipes.

He shrugged, raised one hand in a caustically good-humored salute, and slowly walked back the way he had come. When he stopped at the first of the spoil-heaps and looked around, the

Pulos had vanished again.

Going down the same way he'd come up, Cord changed his route when he neared the dam and crossed by its parapet, smooth-surfaced and broad enough to carry a truck. He stopped for a moment at its mid-point to look up along the length of the valley. The towering hills around were softened by the first touch of approaching dusk, and framed what seemed a green, tranquil heaven. Keeping it like that until it drowned might yet call for greater effort than he'd first imagined.

Hands in his pockets, face unusually grim, Cord continued on toward the guest house.

2

The Thamaung camp mess hall, the only building in the project to boast a full-length verandah, was already busy when Cord arrived. It was a minute or two before eight P.M. and about a dozen people were clustered inside its doorway, chatting and sipping drinks as they waited to move to the dining room beyond.

'You're certainly prompt!' Henry Lewis' lanky figure swept toward Cord. The project chief's face beamed a smile of welcome and his handshake was enthusiastic. 'Well, I've had word from Rangoon, just as you promised.'

'Satisfied?' asked Cord.

'Completely.' Lewis nodded happily. 'I've full authorization to go ahead with your idea — provided the Pulos agree. Marian and I will get down to details first thing in the morning.' He rubbed his hands briskly together. 'I'm going to be an optimist, Cord; I think this will work out. Now, let's get you a drink. What would you like?'

Cord settled for whisky and was pleasantly surprised when it came topped with ice. But before he could do more than taste it, Lewis whisked him on the start of a round of introductions to the rest of the project staff. They finally arrived at the faraway corner where Marian Frey was talking to two men Cord hadn't seen before.

'Well now.' Lewis beamed. 'You've already met Marian . . . '

Cord greeted the brunette with open admiration. She had changed from shirt and slacks to a princess dress in a lightweight oatmeal tweed. She had a white wool cardigan draped over her shoulders. Freed from its ponytail, her dark hair was brushed back to frame her face in soft, gleaming waves.

'Two more people for you to meet, the last, I think,' said Lewis briskly. 'Dr. Holst, our physician, from Norway . . . ' Cord shook hands with Holst, a grizzled, portly figure whose cream drill suit retained a faint whiff of antiseptic. 'And Mr. North, who's — well — let's say a regular visitor, eh Maurice?'

North smiled in agreement. He was about forty, tall, with a rugged athletic build, which added extra tragedy to the fact that the left sleeve of his jacket was empty and pinned discreetly to his side.

'We've been hearing about your meeting with the Pulos,' said North, his voice a slow, natural drawl. 'Nice strategy.'

Marian Frey gave a nod of heartfelt agreement. 'I hope to have a busy time ahead. But for once I'm glad, very glad.'

'Hmm. Better you hear the villagers' answer first, Marian,' growled Dr. Holst, bringing his native Scandinavian caution into play. 'It never pays to be confident too early.'

'There's also such a thing as pessimism,' protested Henry Lewis, a frown of annoyance crossing his face. 'What do you think, Maurice? You've worked with Pulos longer than any of us. How do you think they'll react?'

North gave a shrug. 'It should come off

all right. I'll be surprised if it doesn't.'

'You work in the valley?' queried Talos, finding it hard to put a label on the man.

'Work?' North grinned as he took a battered silver cigarette case from his pocket and flicked it open. 'I'm practically unemployed at the moment. I manage the old ruby mine up at Ronul until such time as the new lake gives it a decent burial.'

'Any heartaches about losing the mine?' Cord took one of the cigarettes, lit it, and waited for an answer.

'Heartaches!' North found the idea amusing. 'Tell him, Marian.'

'Well . . . ' She pondered. 'Let's say it's generally agreed you had the valuator blind drunk when he fixed the company's compensation figure.'

'All done for the good of the stockholders,' chuckled North. 'They've had to wait long enough for any sort of a dividend.'

'Your company did pretty well,' Lewis agreed mildly.

'Pretty well!' Dr. Holst snorted at

the words. 'The mine was practically abandoned when the Thamaung scheme was announced. It was only kept going so that compensation would be paid.'

'Let's say it might have been temporarily closed,' soothed North. 'Ever seen a ruby mine, Cord?'

'Not so far.'

'Then come out first chance you get,' the one-armed mine manager invited him. 'We're practically shut down, but I can still show you the general layout.'

'What happens when the mine floods?' Cord asked. 'Does the firm go prospecting for another location?'

'Not around here,' said North emphatically. 'It would be a waste of time. When Ronul began to play out about two years back, we ran a geological survey over the area. It drew a blank. You need to hit a pretty exact type of crystalline limestone before you've a chance of meeting a ruby vein, and Ronul seems to have been a freak on its own. Most of the big ruby mines are further south, in the Shan states. No, once you've got that tunnel through and start making your little lake,

I'll be heading for Rangoon and looking for an office job.'

They talked on until the dining-hall doors swung open, and then followed the others through. Two long tables were set and ready, and most of the project staff were already at their regular places. Cord found himself placed near the head of one table, with Marian Frey opposite, Lewis on his right, and Dr. Holst on his left. North had attached himself to a group at the other table, and the seat on Marian's right was taken by a solemn-faced Burmese who was resident chief draftsman.

Roasted pork served with sweet potatoes, eggs, and the inevitable rice was the main course. Dr. Holst, a considerable trencherman, barely spoke, until a scraping of chairs at the other table announced two more arrivals.

'The Prinettis — late as usual,' he grunted.

Cord glanced around. Prinetti, out of overalls and in a linen suit one size too small for him, was talking volubly to the plump, fair-haired woman at his side. She was middle-aged, with a calm, bright face.

'Be fair, Doctor,' protested Marian. 'You know they're having trouble getting young Victor to sleep these nights.'

'Not my fault.' Dr. Holst forked at his plate. 'The brat is teething. I gave them a bottle for him — guaranteed to knock out an elephant. But does his mother give it to him? Like most nurses, she thinks she knows better!'

Cord chuckled. 'Any other families here?'

'Just the Prinettis,' said Lewis.

'A special dispensation?'

The project chief reddened a little. 'Well, yes and no. Prinetti is a topnotch foreman and I wanted him. His wife is a good nurse . . . '

'But strong-minded,' growled Dr. Holst.

There was still an empty chair on Marian Frey's left. 'More people still to come?' Cord asked.

'Two. Sometimes they make their own arrangements.' Lewis gave a slightly disapproving sigh. 'Young Andy Donaldson, the radioman, and Lona Marsh, my secretary. You perhaps noticed her this afternoon?'

A full-blossomed figure and that long black hair — he'd noticed all right. Lona Marsh was one more example of the flamboyantly attractive women who often emerged from a blend of races.

'I saw her,' Cord agreed. 'It sounds a pleasant situation for Donaldson.'

Marian Frey answered from across the table, a defensive edge creeping into her voice. 'Not the way some people might think. Lona's not a fool.'

'Gossip is inclined to thrive in a place like this,' murmured Lewis apologetically. 'But they're both excellent young people.' He glanced around, anxious to change the subject. 'Marian and Lona share a bungalow, of course. They're the only two women on the staff, apart from Mrs. Prinetti.' He gave a weak laugh. 'Three women are enough, eh, Holst?'

The Doctor mumbled agreement through a full mouth.

After the meal was finished, the project staff drifted back toward the verandah.

Henry Lewis quickly excused himself and went off. Cord was standing alone by the doorway when the Prinettis came toward him.

'Signor Cord.' The bearded foreman laid a proud arm around his wife's shoulders. 'This is Anna. I have been telling her about this afternoon.'

'And also about his foolishness in going into the tunnel,' said Anna Prinetti with a despairing shake of her head. She turned her keen blue eyes toward Cord. 'You went up there too, later. I was at the surgery window. You crossed below the dam.'

'I went up, but I didn't get into the tunnel,' said Cord ruefully. 'The Pulos didn't seem to like the idea.'

'That will be over by tomorrow,' Prinetti declared expansively. 'I have a sense for these things.'

'You have a sense? Huh!' His wife tugged at his arm. 'I have a sense that if we don't get back, our son will have escaped from his cot.' She smiled at Cord. 'He is a handful, that child, just like his father.'

'Maybe we better go,' Prinetti agreed meekly.

Cord watched them leave, then strolled out to the verandah. Above him, the sky was a deep, dark velvet with a bright twinkling of stars. A yellow moon was emerging from behind a slow-moving patch of cloud. Somewhere not far off there were crickets chirping, and a faint reek of smoke drifted over from the Pulo village.

'Wondering what's going on over there?' Marian Frey had come up quietly beside him, with North close at her elbow. 'Even once the Pulos make up their minds they'll still talk for hours.'

'As long as they give the right answer I don't care if they talk all night,' Cord told her.

'I need that answer too,' said North. 'The sooner our mine is flooded, the sooner I can leave. I'll hear what's happened from my lads in the morning, maybe even before you get the word.' He held his hand out to Cord. 'I'll wish you luck now, before I leave.'

'You're going?' Marian showed her surprise as the two men clasped hands. 'It's still early.'

'But I'm still clearing up the company accounts,' North reminded her with a grimace. 'The job's got to be done, before the auditors get too restless. Good night, Marian.' He bent and gave her a light kiss on the cheek, nodded to Cord, then left the verandah and walked across to where a truck stood parked, a Burmese driver lounging patiently behind the wheel. As soon as North had boarded it, the truck's headlights blazed on, its engine came to life, and the vehicle pulled away into the night.

'He hasn't far to go,' said the girl absently. 'Ronul is only about an hour's drive up the valley.'

'You've been at the mine, Marian?'

'Yes, often.' She saw the flicker of interest in his eyes, and answered it with a quiet firmness. 'Don't jump to conclusions. There are two things you should know about Maurice North. He lost his arm leading one of Wingate's Chindit columns through these hills during the war. The other thing about him is that he happens to be the friendly type. He holds open house for any of us who go up his way, with no strings attached.'

'I didn't ask.'

'But now you know.'

Talos rubbed his chin. 'I've a feeling I should start again. What do you think?'

She looked at him for a moment, then met his slow grin with an answering twinkle. 'All right.'

'Mind if we walk, then? How about down toward the river and back?'

'Fine.' She fell into step with him as they left the verandah. 'Lona should be back at our place by then. Henry Lewis usually arrives at the radio hut about eleven and gets Andy to tune in to some of the shortwave news bulletins. Lona moves clear before he arrives.'

'Handy arrangement.'

They moved on at a leisurely pace through the shadowed buildings.

'Tell me about North,' Cord said, 'has he ever had any trouble up at the mine?'

'You mean from Nam Ree?' She tossed a loose lock of hair back from her forehead. 'Not according to anything I've heard. But there was a story that he met Nam Ree some time back, and arranged to pay him so much a year if he'd stay clear of the mine and make sure other people did, too.'

'What's politely known as the protection racket,' mused Cord.

'Except that Maurice made the first approach. If that's what happened, I'd call it a business deal. There are plenty of other armed bands roaming around North Burma.'

Cord nodded. It was common knowledge — these groups of ragged men hiding in the hills. Some of them had been hunted for more than a decade. There were Chinese Nationalist soldiers who'd hopped across the border when the Communists took over in China. Then — the other side of the coin — there were Burmese Communists, outlawed in their own country, lying low, keeping in touch with Peking's wishes. That left diehard bands of Kachins, Karens, and the rest from Burma's racial pockets — many with their own crazy ideas of an independence which would amount to a patchwork quilt of village republics.

'Marian, how would you rate the Pulos if it came to real trouble?'

She shrugged. 'You've seen them — and Nam Ree, too, according to Henry Lewis. Even right here in the village there are probably plenty of weapons hidden in the roof thatches. They might fight; they might be back growing rice the next day.'

'And Nam Ree?' He kept coming back to this small-time hill rebel. 'How much do you know about him?'

'Only a little, and most of that from Captain Paya. Nam Ree is a Pulo, you know that. He won a scholarship from the mission school, then came back to the valley as a school-teacher. When the war started, he joined the army; he ended up a captain in the Burma Rifles.'

'And after that?'

'He came back to Thamaung after a time and — well — he became caught up in politics and wouldn't take no for an answer.'

Cord gave a slow nod. 'It's happened before. How many men does he have?'

'About fifty. Usually they raid outside the district, then come back here to rest.' She shrugged. 'Captain Paya has a company and a half of motorized infantry at Nanshu. But Nam Ree knows both the hills and the army. He can do pretty much what he likes.'

'Paya says that?'

She laughed. 'No. But everybody else does.'

They walked on for a little way in silence. The project camp lay behind them, and on ahead the moonlight glinted on the high, smooth wall of the dam. The rippling sound of water reached their ears.

'Like to tell me about yourself for a change?' asked Cord. 'I'm interested.'

'Let's see,' she treated the question with friendly tolerance. 'I'm an only child, I took a degree in sociology at London University; my father is a lawyer and my mother runs local church bazaars. What the experts would call a 'conventional middle-class background,' I suppose. Oh — and I've been on U.N. staff for three years. Satisfied?'

'It still leaves gaps — for instance, why you're out here.'

She shrugged. 'I had the qualifications and it sounded like a useful job. The hardest part was persuading the Appointments Board that I didn't see it all as a shortcut to collecting a husband.' She laughed aloud. 'One old dear among them kept warning me about the 'lustful influence' in a camp full of men.'

'Any lust in sight?'

'I'm not in the market.' She took the cigarette he offered, her cupped hand briefly touching his as she shielded his lighter's flame from the wind. 'Heard enough?'

He nodded.

From where they stood, the night sky softened the outline of the towering Dolpha Ridge to a vague, dark silhouette. A voice shouted somewhere in the distance, the sound thin and quickly lost.

'It's getting chilly.' She wriggled deeper into her cardigan. 'Let's get back.'

She didn't stop him as he took her arms and pulled her gently toward him. He kissed her and her lips were soft, moist, and — hell — he thought with a twinge of annoyance, neutral was the only word that came near to classifying her reaction.

'Nice.' The gray eyes were more amused than angry. 'But I told you, I'm not in the market.' She waited until he let her go. 'Mind if we head back now?'

They began to retrace their steps.

'Talos is a Greek name, isn't it?' she asked casually.

'Cretan — out of mythology,' he agreed.

'It's unusual. Did your family have some link with Crete?'

'No.' He tried to leave it at that.

She glanced at him again, more amused than angry. 'Better at asking than answering, aren't you? Go on — I'm interested in people.'

'There's not much to tell.' Cord put

a quiet discouragement into the words. She had touched the one raw spot in his makeup; the years didn't always heal, and he still found it difficult to talk about it.

'Hmm.' She raised an expressive eyebrow. 'I'm disappointed. You didn't seem the type who'd take it as a personal insult that . . . '

'That you're not on the market?' He grinned and ambled on. 'People shouldn't jump to conclusions. You said that, remember?'

In another couple of minutes they had reached her bungalow. It was a slightly larger version of Cord's guest hut, and no light shone from the windows.

'Looks like your roommate is still on the loose,' said Cord.

She chuckled. 'Lona can take care of herself. I wouldn't worry.'

'Marian . . . ' He stepped in front of her as she turned to leave.

'Well?'

'You work among the Pulo villages more than anyone. How do I get to talk to Nam Ree?'

Her half-opened lips showed surprise for a moment. 'Captain Paya's been trying to arrange that for himself long enough.'

'But I'm not Paya. All I want is to talk to Nam Ree, alone.' A fresh earnestness came into his voice. 'Could you get a message out to him?'

She hesitated, then nodded. 'Yes, I think so — in the morning. There should be at least a couple of people in Frajon who still trust me — and that's about all I'd need. What's the message?'

'Will he meet me and talk.'

'All right, I'll try.'

He waited until she'd gone into the bungalow. Then he headed back, walking slowly across the silent, darkened compound. Halfway toward the guest hut he stopped in the shadow of a long, low storage shed, as the quick pad of hurrying feet came toward him.

Lona Marsh passed quickly by without noticing him. He grinned. Lewis' secretary seemed in a hurry to get home. If that meant that the project chief had found her still in the radio hut and had scorched her tail feathers wasn't really his business. The Anglo-Burmese girl was certainly attractive, but her roommate interested him more. Marian Frey might say she wasn't in the market, but any good salesman was prepared for some initial consumer opposition.

Once he'd reached the guest hut he made a minimum of preparation for the night, then undressed and slipped naked under the bed's single sheet and blanket. He switched off the light and lay there in the darkness, hands clasped behind his head. After a moment or two he heard a faint, high-pitched droning in the room. A mosquito had come to life. Well, it wouldn't bother him. Mosquitoes never did.

A few wheels had begun turning, he mused. The results could be interesting — and if Marian could set up a meeting with Nam Ree, that would be best of all.

Marian Frey — his mind wandered around her image, recalling those cool, disconcerting gray eyes and her matter-of-fact attitude — if he wanted to kiss her she might as well get it over with, she seemed to feel. But he remembered, too, that earlier incident in Lewis' office, the way she'd flushed with anger at the idea of troops coming into Thamaung Valley.

'A conventional middle-class background.' That had been her own wry summary. She was the type who probably regarded U.N. work as a jet-age crusade. Maybe it was; it would have to do, anyway, until a better notion came along.

Halfway asleep, he considered Marian again. She hadn't liked it when he'd sidestepped her questions. How to explain that his own background somehow still hurt him in the telling. Not that he'd any real reason to feel sorry for himself. He had money in the bank; he ate all he wanted; he was healthy and enjoyed life . . .

Quite a change from the scrawny, blank-eyed kid he'd been when an Allied officer called Andrew Beck — the same Andrew Beck who now ran Field Reconnaisance — had found him in a civilian internment camp in Shanghai after the Japs had surrendered. He'd been eight years old and alone in the world, his only real friends a White Russian ex-colonel and a Eurasian taxi-dancer from Bombay.

How had he gotten there? That was the real blank. He still couldn't remember anything of life before the camp. The Japs had brought him in, and the scar still on his face had been an open wound when he'd arrived. He hadn't even known his own name, and the only clue was that his ragged shirt had had 'P. Cord' sewn neatly into the neckband.

Andrew Beck had solved the problem. He'd traced back through the records to a British family named Cord who'd been among a shipload of civilians trying to escape before the fall of Hong Kong. The ship had been sunk, with no trace of survivors. But now there was one, Peter Cord, orphan, no known relatives — only Andrew Beck, who took him out of the camp and promptly re-christened him 'Talos.'

Cord smiled to himself in the darkness of the room. That Cretan myth was almost the first thing Beck had taught him, next to how to wear shoes and not to speak with his mouth full. How Daedalus, the same man who tried to fly with feather wings, had built a giant bronze robot for King Minos. Incorruptibly faithful, untiringly reliable, the robot had patrolled the shores of Crete with fire spouting from its mouth as it maintained law and order. It had chased off pirates on occasion, one of them a fellow called Jason, who'd been out looking for a Golden Fleece.

Cord could still feel a fascinated wonderment at Beck's calculated, long-term vision on that day they'd first met. By training, by education, by background, he'd set out to create a new Talos, a man brought up to regard the world as his family tree, insulated against all other loyalties.

Sometimes Cord regretted it, which probably meant the experiment hadn't quite succeeded. But even Andrew Beck couldn't alter the fact that he was flesh and blood.

The mosquito throbbed near the window of the guest hut. As Cord slid into sleep, his last thought was again of Marian Frey. What would she have said about it all . . . ?

* * *

Which of two reasons woke him first he couldn't be certain — the feeling that something was tickling against his throat or the dawning knowledge that the room light was burning above him. Cord stirred drowsily, and the tickle became a thin, hard line pressing lightly against him. He levered open his eyes, then suddenly held every muscle of his body rigidly still. Myi Teri was looking down at him, and the sharp edge of the Pulo headman's *dah* rested on his neck.

'*Kaung bey*!' Myi Teri nodded with quiet satisfaction. 'Even now we seek no violence, Mr. Cord.' One calloused brown hand checked quickly under the pillow against the possibility of a weapon. 'Still, we would be fools to leave anything to chance.' The knife blade lifted. 'Sit up, please.'

Cord obeyed. There were two other villagers in the room, one of them the burly giant with the gold earring. Both had *dahs*, but what mattered was that the big man had a rifle and a cartridge bandolier. Cord risked a glance at his watch; it was almost two A.M.

'I suppose there's a reason for this,' Cord said with cautious politeness.

'There is a reason.' Myi Teri's voice held a weary bitterness. 'Did you think you could bring soldiers here in the night without us knowing? Did you imagine that all your fine talk and new promises would lull us to sleep?'

'Soldiers?' Cord fought the last fragment of sleep from his mind and stared at the headman. 'What soldiers?'

A guttural snarl came from the man with the rifle and the butt of the weapon swung threateningly.

Myi Teri pushed it aside. '*Ma ne* — there is little time left, Mr. Cord. But we know the soldiers are coming to the Thamaung *ching* and that they come to force us to work.' He sucked his teeth in disgust. 'Can no outsider be trusted?'

'Nobody sent for troops,' Cord protested. 'If you've had another tip from Nam Ree, then this time he's wrong.'

The headman hit him open-handed across the face. The blow stung — and the Pulo's anger boiled to the surface.

'They are up on the mountain road, and it is not Nam Ree alone who has seen them. If his men had not blocked the road so that it will take time before their lorries get through, the soldiers would be here by now.'

Cord felt his stomach muscles tighten. 'But that still doesn't mean we asked them to come,' he protested.

Myi Teri looked at his hand. 'Until tonight it is a long time since I struck a man, Mr. Cord. Stay silent and listen, or perhaps I must do more. We know the man Lewis sent for the soldiers. Well, we have taken ten of your people . . . ' He saw the expression which crossed Cord's face and shook his head. 'But we are not savages. They have come to no harm,

except those
their way to
here becaus
serve us bes
come that
tunnel —
people we

'Hell, m
doing?' C
a fool. Ta
the army
some mixup,
you don't let these peop
heading straight for a jail sentence!'

'We are not a people who act lightly.' The Pulo headman's voice was slow and grave. 'Tell the soldiers. We have these ten; we are armed; we have food and water. Our women and children have gone into the forest — and if they are harmed, we will know. Mr. Cord, we will release your people and come back to the village only when you have sent away the soldiers, all the outsiders who work here, and their machines. That — and when you can give us proof that there will be no more work on the tunnel until the agree to it.'

. . .'

yi Teri jerked his head or, and the other Pulos 'This time we must show l not be treated as fools or

three men went out. When the had closed, Cord was already mbling out of bed, pulling on his othes, cursing whatever fool had started this ball rolling. As soon as he could, he was out of the guest hut, heading blindly toward the police post, past silent buildings where here and there a glow of light from an opened door marked the living quarters the Pulos had visited.

He stopped, uncertain, near the project office block.

'Hey — Mr. Cord!' The hoarse, cautious voice hailed him suddenly from the shadows.

Cord turned, and recognized the short wiry figure who stood there, a heavy metal wrench held at the ready in one hand.

'I think they've gone, Andy.'

Clad in pajama trousers and an old jacket, the radioman joined him, his manner grim. 'I don't know what's goin' on, Mr. Cord. But they've made a helluva fine job o' wreckin' my transmitter.'

'Andy,' Cord gripped the young Scot tightly by the arm, 'did you send a radio message to Nanshu asking for troops?'

'The transmitter's smashed. I just told you, man!'

'I meant earlier tonight, did you send a message for Lewis asking for help?'

'No.' Andy Donaldson showed his bewilderment. 'Look, all I know is I heard a row in the room next to mine, had an idea what was happenin', and baled out the back window.' He hefted the wrench. 'I found this. Thought it might come in handy.'

'Seen anyone else?'

'Aye, the girls are all right. I wanted them to stay wi' me, but they went to see if the Prinettis were okay.'

'Right.' Cord gnawed his lip for a moment. 'You show me the way to Prinetti's place. Then head for the police post and see what's happened there. But watch your step.'

'Aye, I'll do that,' grunted Donaldson. 'I'm no' stickin' my neck out to give one of these lads a practice wi' his *dah* knife.'

Donaldson gave him brief directions and they parted. Cord hurried on, shoved past a pair of huddled, frightened workmen, and located the Prinetti house by the blaze of lights from its windows. He threw open the door, went in, and next moment made a lightning duck as Lona Marsh swung at him with a heavy brass candlestick.

'Take it easy, Lona!'

'Mr. Cord . . . ' She lowered the candlestick with a sigh. Her voice rose. 'Marian, here's someone else!'

Marian Frey came out of the back room of the little house. Like her companion, she wore a raincoat belted over her pajamas. Her face pale, she showed him what she had in her hand. It was a piece of torn sheet, heavily bloodstained. 'They've all been taken, Talos, even the child . . . '

'Did the Pulos come your way?' Cord looked around the room, seeing the smashed ornaments, the overturned chair, the other signs of a short furious struggle.

'Yes. But just to tell us to keep out of the way until they'd gone.' It was Lona who answered. Her long black hair hung down her back in a plaited pigtail. And she still gripped her make-shift club.

'We met Andy Donaldson, and we've seen Dr. Holst. Have all the others . . . ' Marian left the question unfinished, her expression dazed.

'Probably all taken,'Cord told her. 'Myi Teri told me a crazy story about Lewis bringing in troops. That's what sparked this off.'

'Troops! But we agreed . . . ' She turned to the other girl. 'Lona, did you know?'

'No.' Lewis' secretary gave a firm, negative shake of her head.

'You were with Andy Donaldson most of the evening at the radio hut, weren't you?' Cord didn't wait for an answer. 'Did he say anything about calling

Nanshu — or did you see Lewis there?'

Her lips tightened, but she again shook her head. 'Andy said nothing, and I left before Mr. Lewis was due.'

'I told you most o' that already,' growled Donaldson's voice from the doorway. He came into the house, giving Cord an angry glare. 'Look, I said I didn't use that radio, an' I meant it.'

Cord shrugged. 'Sorry, Andy. Did you get to the police post?'

'Aye, and found them trussed up like chickens. The Pulos caught them half asleep. Anyway, I cut a couple o' them loose, then came back here.' The radioman suddenly remembered how he was dressed, flushed, and edged back toward the door. Then he stopped, gave a whistle of surprise, and pointed out toward the hills.

Cord crossed to the window, saw for himself, and gave a groan. There were headlights moving on the mountain road, probably a dozen vehicles driving fast toward them.

'It still wasn't me,' said the Scot awkwardly. 'Well, I'll be back.' He disappeared into the night.

* * *

Ten minutes later Captain Paya's jeep led a battle-ready convoy into the Thamaung compound. Beret set at a jaunty angle, a Sten gun in the crook of one arm, the soldier jumped down and shouted an order to his steel-helmeted driver. Behind the jeep the first of the army trucks rumbled in and halted, its men piling out and spreading into line. As the other trucks arrived, the pattern was repeated. Tense and ready, Paya strode forward to where Cord stood waiting in front of a huddle of half-dressed, still bewildered camp workers. 'What is the situation, Mr. Cord?' Paya demanded.

'I'll ask you something first,' snapped Cord. 'Who the hell told you to come here with these men?'

The soldier blinked. 'Lewis, of course; he radioed. He said the Pulos were getting out of hand.' He looked around, uncertain. 'As military commander it is my duty to take control . . . '

'The Pulos didn't get out of hand until they heard you were coming.' Cord clenched his hands by his side, watching the heavily-armed infantry beginning to fan out from the convoy. 'Nam Ree tipped them off. They rounded up Lewis and just about everyone else.'

'But the detail I left here . . . ' Paya glared around the group behind his men and saw the one he wanted. 'Sergeant!'

The disheveled n.c.o. who'd been in charge of the Thamaung police post came forward, biting his lips. A growl from Paya brought him rigidly to attention, and a few snapped questions and hesitant answers put the thunder-faced officer in the picture. He dismissed the man with a final glare and turned back to Cord.

'They were surprised! Idiots! A few villagers with *dahs* and a handful of old rifles and shotguns.' He pursed his lips. 'Well, they are better armed now. They took every weapon there was at the post. I'll have every last one of that guard court-martialed . . . '

'It wouldn't have happened if you hadn't come,' Cord snarled back at him, his face tight with anger. 'Or if you had to come, if you'd made it a blasted sight quicker.'

'Can you fly trucks over a rock slide?' Paya was also in no mood for courtesies. 'They blocked the road and we had to clear it. Where is Lewis?'

'Being held at the tunnel, like the rest.' Cord grabbed the soldier's arm. 'Look, one thing you can't do is go charging up that hill. Myi Teri talked to me. If the army comes too close, then . . . '

'The hostages.' Paya gave a brusque nod. 'I am not a fool, Mr. Cord. But there are some things I must do. For a start, we need a picket line of men down beside the dam and along the river line. Another platoon will check through the village.' He glanced at the group of civilians and shrugged. 'While I do that, you can get these people in order and find out who is missing. We can argue later about what must be done.'

'Right.' While Paya stormed across to his waiting men, Cord turned to the handful standing near him. 'Everybody get dressed, then gather down at the staff mess hall. Open it up, and if there's a cook left, start him working.'

In twenty minutes time he faced the facts. Out of the Thamaung headquarters staff of fourteen only the two girls, Dr. Holst, and Andy Donaldson had been left behind. Holst had escaped because he'd been away from his bungalow when the Pulos arrived. He'd been at the truck drivers' quarters attending a man who'd suddenly come down with fever. For the rest, all of Paya's police post detail and all but four of the imported work gang were accounted for — and the missing quartet could safely be regarded as hiding or still running. On the credit side, too, the only sign of spilled blood was in Prinetti's house. But taking the Italian foreman's wife and child meant that the villagers held twelve captives, not the ten Myi Teri had declared.

Captain Paya, his first-stage tasks complete, sent a runner to Cord with the message that he was at the project radio hut. Cord followed the soldier back, and found Andy Donaldson there ahead of him, a stubborn cast to his mouth as he helped Paya examine the wrecked equipment.

'They used an axe, I think,' said Paya, nodding a greeting. 'Still, it is of little importance. I have a radio truck with my convoy, we've opened a link with Nanshu base.'

'Great,' said Donaldson bitterly. 'But what the hell do we do now, eh?'

'Nothing before daylight,' said Cord wearily. 'There's too big a risk involved.'

'For once, I agree.' Captain Paya dusted down a chair and lowered himself into it with a sigh. 'Just one man going up that hill in this darkness might panic those villagers. And a panic might have — well — unfortunate consequences. Already they are probably beginning to realize what they have done. They will be worried — and their actions unpredictable. But there is something we can talk about, you and I and Donaldson.' His broad face was grave, his voice puzzled. 'If the Pulos were on the brink of going back to work as I'm told, then why did Lewis ask for help?'

'Andy says he didn't,' said Cord.

'And I can ruddy well prove it,' snorted the radioman. He slammed the opened pages of the transmitter log down before them. 'Check for yourselves. There's the last three signals I handled. This one was for Mr. Cord to Rangoon, timed 17:40. There was an incoming cable for Mr. Lewis two hours later; and then the last message was at 19:50, an outgoing plain-language supply requisition.'

'You did nothing else all evening?'

'Well . . . ' Donaldson ran his fingers through his hair. 'Och, there was the usual. I tuned into the Singapore news bulletin for Lewis just before eleven. Once he'd heard it he left, an' I locked up for the night and went off to my quarters.'

'The signal came from here,' Paya insisted. 'I have the details. Thamaung transmitter called up Nanshu base at 23:50. The message was in plain-language Morse. I have checked with our signal team — call sign, procedure, everything was as usual.'

Cord closed the logbook and shook his head, unconvinced. 'You've been trying to trace a pirate transmitter lately, haven't you?'

The soldier stiffened and his face hardened. 'Knowing that means you've talked to Donaldson before. Well, yes, we are. But it is low-power, faint; it is a different matter.'

'It might not be,' mused Cord. 'Still, let's look at this another way. Andy, according to you, if the signal came from your transmitter it must have been after you'd locked up and gone away. Who else in camp could operate the set?'

Donaldson sighed impatiently. 'Henry Lewis could, after a fashion. Nobody else.'

'How many keys are there to the hut?'

'I've got one . . . ' Donaldson hesitated.

'And Lewis has the other?' prodded Cord.

'Aye.'

'The outside door was smashed in when we arrived,' said Paya dryly. '*Ma thi-bu* — perhaps Mr. Cord thinks one of the villagers sent the message.'

'What the devil would they want to do that for?' growled Donaldson.

'To make trouble.' Cord frowned at the wreckage, a hazy possibility forming at the back of his mind. 'Andy, what about Lona Marsh?'

The young Scot flushed. 'What about her? She left just before Lewis arrived. Anyway, she can't work a set.'

'You're sure?'

Donaldson fished out a crumpled pack of cigarettes from his shirt pocket, struck a match against the wall of the hut, and took a long draw of smoke. 'Man, I know. I started trying to teach her Morse code for a laugh about a month back and she still can't tap out her own name.' A thought struck him, and he prowled over to the band-tuner on the wrecked receiver. 'Here's something else for both of you to think about. This set is still tuned to Radio Singapore, the way I left it. It would have to be changed to call up Nanshu. If somebody did that, then why bother to change it back?'

Cord shook his head. 'No sense in

guessing, Andy. Not until we know a little more.' He glanced at his watch. It was four-thirty A.M., and he'd long since given up thought of further rest.

* * *

Morning came to the valley as a shrouding gray mist, slow to rise, clinging in patches to the hills and forest, lacing its thin stubborn tendrils along the river's course. From the village side of the dam parapet the view across to Dolpha Ridge was at first a mere smoke-like haze. But gradually, as if some vast projector lens was being brought slowly into focus, shapes and outlines began to harden.

'It is always like this.' Captain Paya strained to look through the binoculars for a moment longer, then laid them aside and massaged his eyes with weary fingers. 'Still, I can see enough.' He flickered a grim half-smile toward Cord. 'So can the ones over there, enough to sight a rifle, my friend.'

'A nice thought.' Cord took a last draw at his cigarette, then stubbed it out. They were inside the small control cabin which stood on the village end of the dam's parapet. Before dawn Paya's men had strengthened its thin walls with sandbags and converted it into a firing post. Three young soldiers squatted beside them, one with a walkie-talkie, his companions each nursing a self-loading rifle. Only a few other soldiers were in sight, spaced at intervals along their side of the river line. But more were near, and a platoon was guarding the mountain road. Another force had been detailed for the age-old tactic of making a show of force along the length of the valley, an antidote to the possibility that more of the Pulos might feel tempted to join the Frajon villagers in their stand.

Paya slouched back against the sandbags with the ease of a man who knows tension pays few dividends. 'Most of the villagers seem to be up around the tunnel mouth. But they've got men around the spoil-heaps. The ones I've seen are keeping low.' He glanced at his watch. 'Eight A.M. — the time you chose. You still don't want me to come?'

Cord shook his head. 'A uniform would be about the last sight they'd welcome.'

'As you wish.' Paya pulled a strand of fiber from one of the sandbags and rolled it into a tiny ball between his fingers. 'A watchful man could learn many useful things up there, useful if we have to finish this the hard way.'

'That's on my mind.' Cord had no particular scruple at the idea. He was going up there trusting for a truce; but hard practicalities had to be served, practicalities which might be needed to reduce violence to a necessary minimum.

'In particular, I want to know if you see this man.' Paya unbuttoned the breast pocket of his combat blouse, took out his wallet, and handed Cord a worn-edged photograph. 'The likeness is an old one and only reasonable, but it is the best we have.'

The head-and-shoulders picture showed a smiling man in army khaki. The young bronze face was round and button-nosed, with high cheekbones. But it was the eyes that clinched the identification, deep-set, strangely magnetic.

'I've seen him already — Nam Ree.'

'You,' the soldier swallowed, 'you saw him? When?'

Cord told him, while Paya's face went through a kaleidoscope of emotions. That the number one rebel in his area should have been making regular public appearances literally within a stone's throw of an army detail and that the Thamaung project team had quietly ignored the fact was almost more than the soldier could bear.

'*Ho'ba* — can all this get any worse?' He was reduced to a mere croak.

'I wouldn't be surprised.' Cord gave him a sympathetic grin and rose to his feet. 'Time to go. I'll be back within the hour.'

'Perhaps.' Paya scratched unhappily under his beret. 'I hope so.'

Outside the sandbagged shelter of the post, Cord felt suddenly alone. He walked out along the broad concrete parapet of the dam, the sound of his footsteps loud in his own ears. He was halfway across the parapet's length, walking steadily, empty hands held purposely away from his sides, before there was any visible reaction from the other end of the dam. First came a shout, then the noisy clamor of a makeshift alarm gong.

Moving without haste, he kept going. On the far side he heard the faint snick of a rifle bolt as he stepped back on the ground again. Where the sound came from he couldn't tell, but it was an eerie sensation, trudging up that hill path, conscious that he had at least one set of rifle sights trained on him at close range and that, across the river, Paya's men were also watching and waiting. As he approached the first of the spoil-heaps, a figure suddenly appeared out of the tendrils of mist.

'*Kaung ba-byi*, Mr. Cord.' Myi Teri came toward him, a revolver stuck awkwardly into the waist of his *loongyi*. 'I thought it was you. Is there an answer for us?'

Cord shook his head. 'Not yet. These things take time — and your men smashed our radio, which makes things more difficult. I've another reason for coming.'

'Destroying the radio was stupidity, but tempers were hot. They found the door locked and that angered them more.' There was a hard dignity in the headman's manner as he invited Cord to walk on. He led the way, saying nothing while they climbed on up the path toward the tunnel camp. Men moved here and there among the spoil-heaps, perched uncomfortably among the rocks, watching them pass in absolute silence. Nearer the tunnel the Pulos had set up their own rough camp, amid the construction materials. Small cooking fires burned; a few men sat eating. At the tunnel mouth two sentries stood on guard.

Myi Teri stooped and faced his visitor. 'Now, Mr. Cord, why have you come?'

'To see for myself that the people you took are unharmed, and to ask why, when you have so many, you have to hold a woman and her child.'

'The nurse and her little *ka-ley* . . . ' The headman pursed his lips unhappily. 'That was not planned. But her man fought like a madman, and we did not want to kill him, Mr. Cord. We took his wife and son, and he stopped fighting.'

'We found blood.'

'Some of his, some of ours. But he is well; they are all well.'

'A woman, a child, and an injured man.' Cord rubbed his chin. 'Up here they could be more trouble than they are worth to you. If they were allowed to go, then the world outside would see it as a way of showing that you have no quarrel with such people.'

Myi Teri pondered the point, undecided for a moment. Then he nodded. 'They can go back with you. But the others stay.'

'There is another thing I must do before there can be any more talk about the dam.' Cord saw the headman's eyes harden again, but kept on. 'I must know why the soldiers came. The only way to do that is to talk to Henry Lewis. Until I have seen him, nothing can be done.'

He'd expected to have to argue his way through. But Myi Teri merely grunted and gestured him on again toward the tunnel. At its mouth one of the two sentries ran his hands over him in a brief, perfunctory search. The man nodded, and they went in.

Twenty yards inside the tunnel's gloom two small kerosene lamps threw a pool of light, glinting on the steel rails of the tub track and illuminating the figures of the group of men who sat listlessly on the cold rock floor. The hostages looked up as they heard the approaching, echoing footsteps, then began scrambling to their feet.

A murmured order from Myi Teri sent the two Pulo guards forward. A moment later Henry Lewis was pushed toward the tunnel mouth, while the rest of the captives were held back.

'Cord!' Lewis stumbled, then steadied himself. The project chief was unshaven, tunnel grime smeared his clothes, and anxiety showed in every line of his face. 'Are we getting out of here?'

'Not yet.' Cord looked past him to where the other hostages were waiting hopefully. One or two showed signs of rough handling, but otherwise they seemed unhurt. 'You know why the Pulos did this, Lewis?'

'They told us.' Lewis shook his head. 'The whole thing's crazy.'

'Did you radio Captain Paya to bring in troops?'

'Me?' Lewis raised his clenched fists in despair. 'No I didn't. I've already told Myi Teri that Paya must have acted on his own decision.'

'He says he got a radio call for help,' said Cord softly.

Beside him, Myi Teri's face twisted in an expression of unadulterated disbelief. 'Does it matter which of them is lying? The result is the same — the soldiers are here.'

'It does.' Cord looked at the headman with a steady determination. 'It does, if you meant it when you said that you didn't want bloodshed.'

Myi Teri frowned, then shrugged. 'Talk if you want.'

'Right.' Cord wasted no time. 'Lewis, according to Andy Donaldson, you left the radio hut after you'd heard the Singapore news broadcast. Did you go back for any reason?'

'No.' Lewis shook his head. 'Why should I? I knew Andy was locking up behind me and ready to leave.'

'He says he did, and the door was still locked when Myi Teri's men reached it,' Cord agreed. 'But the signal to Paya almost certainly came from there. You can use a Morse key and you had the second key to the radio hut.'

'You think I might have sent that message. You really do, don't you?' Henry Lewis' shocked reaction had to be genuine.

'Somebody did,' Cord reminded him. 'Where was that door key last night?'

'In my office, where it always is, locked in my desk.' The project chief seemed close to tears of rage and humiliation. 'Cord, why would I do anything like this? You're talking about my dam, my tunnel . . . ' He broke off, shaking his head.

Cord gnawed his lip and turned back to Myi Teri. 'You heard for yourself. The camp did not send for soldiers. Have you thought how Nam Ree found out about this so quickly? Couldn't the answer be that it was Nam Ree who sent the message to the army post at Nanshu?'

The Pulo headman gave a harsh, hostile laugh. 'You expect me to believe this? Nam Ree is not here. Even if he was . . . ' He spat expressively on the tunnel floor. 'I think that of your idea — and there has been enough talk.'

Lewis was shoved back to join the other hostages. A moment later and Cord found himself half-pushed, half-guided back out into the open air.

'Leave now,' said Myi Teri curtly. 'Next time you come, it must be to tell us that what we ask is agreed.'

'And Prinetti and his family?'

Myi Teri hesitated, then nodded. 'Take them as I promised.' He barked an order to the nearest of the cluster of villagers who stood watching them, and a handful went off in the direction of the construction huts. They returned shepherding the Prinettis before them. Anna Prinetti came first, her fair hair wispy and uncombed, her arms cradling her small, blanket-wrapped son. Two paces behind them came Prinetti, his head swathed in a rough bandage, his face pale beneath his beard.

Myi Teri looked at the child and his face softened for a moment. 'He is asleep. *Hla* — I will carry him.' He nodded. 'You are going back.'

Anna Prinetti looked down at the child, then at Myi Teri. She found what she wanted in the Pulo's face and allowed him to take the boy from her arms.

'How's the head, Prinetti?' asked Cord.

The Italian foreman gave a weak grin. '*Va bene,* signor. It still goes thump, but that is all. Anna fixed it.'

The woman moistened her lips and attempted a smile. 'He has a thick skull.'

'Well, let's go.' Cord turned to Myi Teri. 'This, at least, shows sense.'

The Pulo gave a grunt and led the way. They followed him down the hill, two of the villagers still in attendance.

Past the spoil-heaps, at the start of the dam parapet, Myi Teri stopped and looked across to the other side of the river and the watching, waiting line of steel-helmeted infantry. 'For me, this is far enough.'

Cord nodded and took the child. The youngster squirmed a little at the change of position, but still seemed half-asleep.

'Signor?' Prinetti hesitated.

'Go on.' He waited until the Italian and his wife had set out along the parapet walkway, then attempted a last plea to Myi Teri. 'You know how to contact Nam Ree. Tell him I want to meet him, that I'll come alone — anywhere he chooses. All I'm seeking is a way to end this trouble.'

The headman said nothing; his face remained impassive.

Cord eased the child into a more comfortable position in his arms and set off along the parapet. Halfway across the three-hundred-yard distance he looked back. Myi Teri hadn't moved, though the two villagers had now vanished from sight. Cord shrugged and went on.

Anna Prinetti and her husband had just reached the sandbagged control cabin, Cord about fifty yards behind them, when the shots smashed out, two, fired in quick succession, the twin report echoing against the hills. Cord froze for an instant, looked over his shoulder, saw Myi Teri had fallen, and began running, his feet pounding on the concrete.

For a long moment the unexpectedness of what had happened seemed to paralyze the Pulos. Then an angry, ragged burst of gunfire spat from the Dolpha Ridge spoil-heaps, while Myi Teri's two companions reappeared out of hiding and dragged their leader back toward shelter.

A bullet whipped past Cord's ear as he raced toward the safety of the control cabin. Another bit the concrete near his feet and whined off in a wild ricochet, while he kept on, forcing the utmost from his leg muscles, crouching low, shielding the child with his body.

A whistle shrilled from the control cabin, and a violent torrent of answering fire lashed out from the sandbagged fox-holes along the river line. Rifles and light automatics raked the spoil-heaps with their fury, then, as Cord stumbled and half-fell into the sandbagged cabin, the whistle shrilled again and the firing stopped. A last few shots barked from the spoil-heaps, but that ceased, and the valley was again silent.

'*Kaung bey* — well done! You seem born lucky, Mr. Cord.' Captain Paya took the child from him. 'We should move back a little way, I think.'

Crouching low, they followed him past the soldiers in the post busy reloading their weapons. From the rear of the cabin he led them quickly into the shelter of the thick clusters of wild purple-flowered rhododendron which grew to the dam's edge. After that it was a short, fast walk to leave the danger area behind.

'This will do.' Paya halted and let Mrs. Prinetti take charge of her son.

'We're in trouble now,' said Cord bleakly.

'If I can find the fool who fired these two shots . . . ' The soldier's face twisted in fury. 'Cord, the order was clear — no firing until I signaled. Even then, it was to be over their heads!' He shoved the beret back from his sweat-streaked forehead. 'Well, at least Myi Teri is probably still alive. I saw him moving as they carried him in.'

'That helps a little,' agreed Cord. 'But I'll take a bet you don't find the man who shot him, Paya.'

'By the time I am finished . . . '

Talos Cord gave a slow shake of his head. 'Maybe it wasn't one of your men. First we have a radio message sent from nowhere, then this — the same pattern, stirring up maximum trouble. Nam Ree isn't at the tunnel camp. But he could be on this side of the river. There's plenty of cover.'

'But why shoot the people he's trying to help?' protested Paya.

Cord had no answer. But he had a thread of an idea which might start him on the way toward the truth — if, first, Dr. Holst and, then, Marian would each play their part.

3

Dr. Holst went out across the dam parapet at ten A.M., black medical bag in one hand, a white handkerchief tied to a stick in the other. From the control post Cord watched a Pulo villager meet the portly physician on the far side, and then doctor and Pulo disappeared from view. Exactly an hour later the plank walkway below the dam blew up with a reverberating roar, despite the fact that the nearest infantry guard point, less than thirty feet away, had seen no sign of movement; and five minutes afterward Holst's lone, stumpy figure trudged back across the dam again.

'Well, how is he?' demanded Captain Paya as soon as the medical man had reached the sandbagged post.

'Myi Teri?' Holst shrugged. 'Alive and angry. The rest can wait. I need a drink.'

They had to follow him like sheep

all the way from the dam to the compound's medical center. Once inside, Holst collapsed with a sigh into a chair, opened the big right-hand drawer of his desk, and took out a bottle and three glasses. 'Recommended stimulant,' he said shortly, pouring a stiff tot of whisky into one glass. 'Help yourselves.' He shoved the bottle toward them, then drained the glass and smacked his lips. 'Well, I've a message for you . . . '

'What about the bullet?' demanded Cord.

'The object of my mercy mission?' Holst grunted, poured himself another drink, and nursed the glass, letting the bright sunlight streaming in the window give the amber liquid a glowing radiance. 'I've got it. Are you drinking or not?' They declined, and he gave a short, mirthless laugh. 'I'd prescribe this on medical grounds. You're going to need it.'

They persuaded him to start at the beginning.

'Well, I won't say they welcomed me with open arms.' He grimaced. 'Not at first, anyway. But I got to Myi Teri eventually and treated him. They've no other casualties.'

Paya gave a nod of satisfaction. The exchange of fire across the river might have been noisy, but his men had also escaped unharmed.

'Bullet took him in the left leg, on the fleshy part of the upper thigh,' said Holst, rolling out the words with clinical deliberation. 'Nice, neat hole, no artery damage, and it missed the bone. He won't walk for a month or so, but that's all. The second shot missed.'

'And the bullet?'

'Impatient, aren't you?' Holst sipped his drink before taking a small wad of cotton from his jacket pocket. 'Must have been fired from fairly long range, otherwise it would have bored through him and kept on going.'

Cord opened the cotton wad, inspected the small bright-tipped bullet that nestled within, and passed it to Paya.

The soldier inspected the metal slug for a moment, then gave his verdict. 'None of my men fired this.' He was considerably relieved. 'They use the new 7.62 mm. ammunition — smaller, with the bullet tapered at the base. This,' he glanced down at his hand, 'this is from a .303 rifle; old stock service ammunition. The aluminum tip is long obsolete.'

Cord nodded. If this bullet hadn't forced its way out through an exit wound, yet hadn't hit bone, then Holst's guess about distance was correct. A .303 rifle bullet left its firing chamber propelled by a pressure of twenty tons per square inch. It still had killing power at three thousand yards.

'Glad you're satisfied,' snorted Holst. 'Well, let's see if the rest makes you as happy. Once I'd patched him up and sneaked that thing into my pocket, Myi Teri gave me a message to bring back. There's only one way to reply to it — you've got three days to blow up the dam.'

'Or else?' Cord stiffened, fearing the inevitability of the rest.

'He didn't go into details,' said Holst. 'Just that he could always blow up the front half of the tunnel and leave Lewis and everyone else inside. He says he'll do that anyway if Paya's men try any attack on him. The rest of it was a long speech about how he was dealing with a pack of — well — jackals was one of the milder descriptions.'

'But you told him there was no order to fire?' Paya clenched the bullet in his fist.

'I told him. With that hole in his leg, he wasn't impressed . . . ' Holst drained the glass again. 'Anyway, he says they won't move from Thamaung at any price now, and the dam has to go. They've got explosives and know how to use them; the plank bridge was a demonstration. But they want us to blast the dam. Makes it more final, they feel.'

'A nice touch,' agreed Cord. He thought of the cable he'd received via Paya's radio truck only half an hour ago. Andrew Beck's reaction to the Pulos' overnight seizure had been a terse, simple order to 'expedite a solution.' It was easy enough to curse the Field Reconnaisance chief sitting on his backside in an air-conditioned room half the world away;

yet if there had been any magic formula waiting to be administered, Beck would have named it.

'Well, what happens next?' demanded Holst.

Captain Paya stirred and scowled at Cord. 'If you ask, my men can take that hill inside fifteen minutes. But . . . '

'But that wouldn't be much of a consolation to Lewis and his men.' Cord shook his head. 'That's out. We've got three days, and we've got to find the best way to use them.' Three days for him to find a way to escape from the vice-like grip of an impossible choice. How could he find a way to tackle these hill villagers; people now confused, desperate, and bitterly unable to trust any outsider.

'I won't say Myi Teri loves me like a brother,' mused Dr. Holst. 'But I've arranged to go back tomorrow and dress his wound again. Let me know if I can play at being postman.'

They thanked Holst, left him, and went out into the compound. The sky above was a clear blue and a light wind was blowing up from the south, stirring and eddying low clouds of earth dust to life. The start of spring in the Kachin Hills was a bounty of pleasure, a gradual build-up of heat before the May rains. Only the dust, red-brown, penetrating, eager for any breeze, mocked the season. Captain Paya rubbed one shoe along the ground, and gloomily contemplated the groove he'd created.

'When they gave me this district to administer I was happy at its happening,' he said heavily. 'Now — a soldier's job is not just to fight, I know that. But do I tell my men to storm the hill, or do I make you blow up that cursed dam? I would be finished either way, and I am too young for the politeness of being retired.' He forced a half-smile. 'Even my health is good.'

Cord gave a sympathetic chuckle. 'Then we'd better keep working. Did you ever meet Nam Ree in his army days?'

Paya shook his head. 'If I had, and if I had known what was ahead, I would have shot him then and there.'

'Let's suppose the army taught him how to operate a transmitter.' Cord saw his words met with limited enthusiasm, but pushed on. 'Let's keep supposing — that he had a way of knowing the Thamaung station's working procedure and sent the radio call that brought you here . . . '

'Why would he do it?' demanded Paya abruptly.

'When I know that, I'll be halfway to a lot more information,' said Cord patiently. 'But let's work on this for now. Can you trace his army record and find out if he had signal training?'

'Yes, there is no problem there.'

'Good.' Cord was thoughtful for a moment. 'Paya, you asked Donaldson to keep a listening watch for an illegal transmitter — no, I'm not suggesting it sent the signal. But you know what that illegal transmitter might mean when you're so close to the Chinese border. Your own military intelligence must keep pretty close tabs on what happens across the border strip. Have they turned up anything out of the ordinary lately?'

The soldier reacted pretty much as he'd feared. A sudden guarded caution fell into place like protective armor. 'That would come under the heading of restricted information, Mr. Cord. Remember, you are both a foreigner and a civilian . . . '

'You think that matters right now?' snapped Cord, his temper fraying. 'We're in this together, aren't we?'

'Perhaps.' Paya chewed his lower lip. 'Just what is this Field Reconnaisance section you come from, Mr. Cord? I think I am beginning to guess.' He shrugged, not waiting for an answer. 'Very well, the latest confidential reports spoke of some troop movements along the Chinese border provinces. But that is always happening. The Chinese trust no one. They do not let their troops settle in one place for any length of time. Of course, if you have some definite pointer . . . '

'No.' Cord looked past the soldier toward the high hills of the Dolpha Ridge. 'Let's leave it for now. Supposing you were to begin an all-out comb through the area, how long would it take to locate Nam Ree's camp?'

'Weeks, maybe longer.' Paya rubbed his chin, obviously feeling the statement justified an explanation. 'There are few paths through these hills, Mr. Cord, and the Pulos are not given to volunteering as guides. That is just the start. The whole Ridge is riddled with caves, many of them interlinked. All we know is that somewhere up there is a place called the Cave of Bats, and that it is there Nam Ree has his base.' He shrugged. 'We have tried, more than once, but never with any luck.'

'He's on his home ground.' Cord nodded. 'You'll let me know about his army record?'

'I will send the signal now.' Thumbs tucked into his webbing belt, Captain Paya wandered off, a wan, care-laden figure compared with the crisp, authoritative individual of not so many hours before.

Cord headed in the opposite direction, toward the project office. A group of workmen sat on the hard, dusty ground in the shaded rear of the staff block opposite, listlessly watching three of their number at a dice game. Each player had a thin wad of kyat notes at his side, a stone on top to prevent the paper money from blowing. They, at least, had time on their hands. Cord went into the project office and along its silent, empty corridor. Lewis' outer office was deserted, but Marian Frey was waiting in the room beyond.

'Where's Lona?' Cord asked.

'With the Prinetti family.' She frowned. 'Talos, I still don't like doing this.'

'You'll like what's happened even less.' He told her Myi Teri's ultimatum, and saw her eyes widen, her face pale with shock. 'Did you get what I wanted?'

Silently she handed over a small, jingling key ring. A tiny brass Buddha was attached to it as a fob and his nostrils caught a vague, lingering trace of perfume.

'Thanks.' He knew she was far from happy. Marian's first reaction when he'd asked her to steal Lona Marsh's keys and meet him in Lewis' room had been one of indignant refusal. He'd talked the brunette around, but that didn't mean she supported the idea. 'I'll check Lona's desk first. Keep an eye on the corridor.'

She gave a reluctant nod, followed him back into the outer office, and stood over at the door. Only one drawer of Lona's desk was locked, and he quickly found the correct key to open it. Inside was a miscellany of items, from a petty cash box to a powder compact and a supply of clean, laundered handkerchiefs. He checked them through, then continued his search. The other drawers held stationery supplies, a pair of old low-heeled shoes, and a notebook which had half its pages filled with the dots and dashes of the Morse alphabet. He read through a couple of pages and gave a flickering grin. Andy Donaldson had been right. Lona's secretarial efficiency didn't appear to extend to telegraphy.

Cord closed and relocked the desk. Its top was bare, except for a small tray containing a few pencils, some typewriter carbons, and a small date stamp.

The filing cabinets and another small cupboard in the room yielded nothing of interest. He nodded to Marian, and they moved back into Lewis' office. The project chief's desk was locked on both sides. Cord tried three keys from Lona's ring, one after the other, without success. The rest were patently useless. He turned to the two wide-mouthed jars lying on the desk. One held cheroots, the other a tangle of paper clips and rubber bands.

'Is this what you want?' Marian came around the desk to stand beside him. She lifted a paper clip, bent one end into a rough hook, inserted it in the right-hand lock, twisted, and the lock opened. She repeated the performance with the other lock, then stood back, her gray eyes mocking him. 'My desk is the same make — and I keep forgetting my keys.'

He gave a rueful shrug, then opened the first drawer on the left. At the front, in an old wooden cigar box, lay a single door key. He hardly needed to read the label attached to it to know he'd found the radio room key, lying where it was always kept, where anybody with a piece of bent wire could have located it.

'Seen enough?' she asked.

'More than enough,' he said grimly. 'I'll bet anything against that paper clip that somebody took Lewis' key last night, somebody who had a pretty close acquantaince with all that went on.'

She still struggled against the idea. 'But why bother returning the key?'

'For the same reason the waveband tuner was moved back to the radio Singapore frequency. To keep us chasing our tails just that little bit longer — because we're talking about somebody still around the camp, somebody the Pulos didn't drag off to the tunnel!'

Her lips tightened. 'Well, it still doesn't have to be Lona.'

'No. But she's a possible,' Cord emphasized. 'She left the radio hut before eleven. I left you about eleven-fifteen, and it was after that when she passed me in the compound. Would she know how easy it was to open this desk?'

'I suppose so.'

'Then she'd time to take the key, give it to — well — let's leave it to somebody else. She could have collected it later from wherever it was hidden and brought it back here. She spends a lot of time with Andy Donaldson, enough to pick up any procedure details which might be needed.'

'What about me?' Marian demanded. 'Couldn't I have done it?'

'I don't see how. I'm part of your alibi and Lona's the rest. You can't return the compliment as far as she's concerned. But Holst might have done it, then had his convenient 'sick' patient to get him out of the way. Come to that, Andy Donaldson's story about getting out a back window could be pretty thin.' He leaned back against the desk. 'I need more help on this, Marian.'

'You mean from outside the valley?' For once, she seemed all in favor.

Cord shook his head. The last thing he wanted to see was a heavy-footed squad from U.N. administration or Burmese officialdom descending on the valley, not when the situation resembled that of walking on eggs. He was relying on Beck to fend off interference for as long as possible.

'Personal help, Marian. I want you to have a talk with some of the truck drivers and find out more about the patient Dr. Holst was called to see. Keep an eye on Lona, too — what she does, where she goes.'

'Anything else?' The brunette resigned herself to her role. 'What about Andy Donaldson?'

That was more difficult. 'I'd like to know if he can use a rifle — or owns one. In fact, I want anything you can dig up about any of their backgrounds.'

She nodded, closed the desk drawers, and used the paper clip to lock them again. 'And you? Where will you be?'

'At Ronul.' Cord gave an almost boyish smile. 'I still want to meet Nam Ree. Your Pulo contacts — well — they aren't available. Myi Teri is in no mood to help. That leaves Maurice North. If he can't pitch in, then I'll really be near the end of the line.' Or the dam, he added mentally.

'I see.' She looked at him steadily, thoughtfully. 'Then give Maurice a message from me. Tell him — tell him, I hope he'll help, even though I'm staying. He'll understand.' She seemed about to say more, but instead gave him a quick nod and went out.

He heard her footsteps along the corridor, then the outer door opened and closed.

Cord stayed where he was long enough to check the map for a route to the ruby mine. Then he folded it, put it in his hip pocket, and left. Outside, the same group were still in their dice game, most of the money had moved toward a thin youngster whose long, snapping fingers practically caressed the dice before each throw. He passed them, walked around to the parking lot, and got aboard the Renault pick-up. He checked the fuel gauge, was pleasantly surprised to find that someone had filled up the tank, then started the engine.

The little truck was purring out of the compound when he spotted a figure with a familiar, bandaged head hurrying toward him. He stopped the Renault and Prinetti finished the last of the distance at a breathless jog trot.

'You going up the valley, Signor Cord?'

'To Ronul,' he told the foreman. 'Everyone all right now?'

'*Si.*' Prinetti grinned. 'Dr. Holst gives me this new bandage; young Victor has his tooth through — everything's fine. I thought maybe you'd like a guide. Nothing for me to do here except get in Anna's way.'

Cord considered the man for a moment, then thumbed toward the passenger seat. 'Hop in.'

Prinetti came around, scrambled into the pick-up's cab, and slouched back happily as the truck began moving again.

'Straight out through the Pulo village,' he directed. 'Then we take the track to the right, that gets us around the dam.'

They drove past the empty, deserted huts. The track was exactly that and nothing more, two parallel strips of broken rutted stone and gravel winding up an avenue cleared through the trees above the village. The pick-up climbed, tires spitting loose gravel from their treads, engine throbbing busily. Prinetti nudged him and Cord looked across to his left. The dam spread below them, a tree-framed picture with the Thamaung River trickling through it in a lazy, sun-silvered flow. Across and almost level with the truck, a few ant-like figures moved around at the tunnel camp on the Dolpha.

A last climbing stretch through the trees and the track leveled before winding down again toward the valley. From there, the route was easy enough to follow. They bumped along, the trees left behind, traveling through open grassland.

Prinetti made a grimly cheerful companion. 'We going to blow up our dam like they want?' he demanded.

'Not unless we have to,' Cord assured him.

'*Buono*.' The Italian scratched thoughtfully at his beard. 'You know what I'd do?' He clutched the dashboard as the springs took a particularly wild bounce. 'Tell them to go to hell. This is a U.N. project, right? Does that size of an outfit let a bunch of backwood *contadini* push them around?'

'They've got Lewis and the others,' Cord reminded him.

Prinetti sniffed. 'Easy. Tell them if anything happens it'll be called murder, and every last one of them'll end up on the end of a rope or whatever the local custom lays down.'

'They let you go,' said Cord, watching the track.

Prinetti chuckled. 'That was a surprise, after what happened. I really bang-bashed a couple of them.' His face clouded. 'But you stop fighting when there's one of those *dah* knives wavin' over your wife an' kid. One thing, though,' he rubbed his head dolefully, 'I don' know what they hit me with after that. Hey, we go left now . . . '

They turned down toward the river, past a handful of Pulo huts and an area of carefully walled rice paddies, each tiny field fed by a rough irrigation channel made of split and hollowed tree trunks. Other tire tracks led to the water's edge, and Cord followed them. The line of the ford was marked by a white post on the opposite bank; the water was broad but only inches deep; and they crossed without trouble, keeping the pick-up in low gear and its engine revving. On the far side the wet, dripping wheels re-emerged to travel along a clearly defined lane through waving expanses of yellow-flowered primula.

'All right, eh?' Prinetti lounged back, large hands folded across his stomach. 'But come this way in just a couple of weeks, signor, an' you would end up in water to your neck. That's when the snow is melting up north, in the mountains.' He scowled. 'Well, we won't be ready for it this year, not now.'

Their route crossed the width of the valley, then they were running close under the continuing shadow of the Dolpha Ridge. Small, distant clusters of thatch-roofed stilt-legged huts perched on the lower hillsides, terraced stretches of cultivation in front of them, the forest beginning immediately behind, a thick luxuriantly leafed mixture of blossoming cherry and stately conifers, dwarfed now and then by a solitary giant coffin tree. Higher still, thin bush and scrub gave way to the bare rock, where soaring pinnacles rose in silhouette like so many Gothic spires.

'You heard that fuss they made about their 'holy *ku*.'' Prinetti thumbed toward the hills ahead. 'It's up there. Jus' a hole in the rock, that's all, but decked out with its little fruit baskets and bowls like a goddamn shrine. Almost as bad as the way they plaster gold leaf over the pagodas down south; get the job of scrapin' one down an' you could net a fortune.' He chuckled. 'I said that to Lona at our place las' night, an' . . . '

'Last night?' Cord took his eyes off the track for an instant.

'*Si*. We were talking about the Pulos, an' . . . '

'When?'

Prinetti shrugged. 'Late on, 'bout eleven. She looked in to see how young Victor was settlin'. Nice girl.'

'How long did she stay?'

'Not long. Ten, fifteen minutes. Jus' long enough to have a glass of wine.' The foreman squinted at him. 'Anything wrong, signor?'

'No.' Cord dedicated a moment's silence to Lona Marsh's new-found alibi. She might still have managed the time to get Lewis' key, but the odds were lengthening against it. 'How far now to the mine?'

'In a minute we begin to climb. Then we are nearly there.' Prinetti looked at him again, puzzled, but saw no encouragement and gave up.

* * *

The ruby is the most valued of all gems, and it is among the strangest. Its radiant red, for instance, is actually two separate colors — carmine and orange. Heat it and it turns green, only to resume its original dress as it cools. Throughout history its main location has been upper Burma, where it has come from a handful of mines so jealously guarded that even their locations were barely known until less than a century ago.

It is mined by three main methods — from cave deposits, from pit mines, and from water mines. All come down to the same thing — digging out gravel and sand and clay, washing it, hoping that a few carats of gem stones are buried somewhere in each ton or so of worthless muck.

Ronul was a cave deposit, an original limestone cavern developed by pick and shovel into a galleried 'loodwin,' a crooked mine, by generations of men who followed its band of crystalline limestone through the unfriendly granite all around. But its prime was long past. Cord's first impression was of a derelict collection of leaf-thatched sheds and rusted ironwork, a raw gash in the hillside rock and an ugly chaos of mounded gravel and mud. The age of some of the mounds could be gauged by the twisted, stunted trees and bushes which pushed through their weed-grown slopes.

Guided by Prinetti, Cord piloted the Renault across the maze of neglected machinery and broken-roofed huts and pulled in beside one of the few buildings which maintained any pretense of pride or use. Built basically in Burmese style, with teak stilts and plank walls, this building was set apart from the usual by its brick chimney and red tiled roof, by a lingering attempt at a rock garden, and the painted iron stairway which led from there to the verandah.

As they arrived, an elderly Pulo woman in a wrap-around gown shuffled to the doorway of the house, looked out, and went back in again. A moment later Maurice North hurried down the stairway toward them.

'First the army, then you two . . . ' The one-armed mine manager greeted them with sober enthusiasm. 'Well, what's the latest at the dam?'

'There's been more trouble. Myi Teri was wounded,' said Cord.

North chewed his upper lip. 'Bad. A couple of truckloads of military passed through here this morning on a patrol up the valley. I got most of what had happened last night from their lieutenant.' He gave an apologetic shrug. 'I wanted to come down, but — well — that sort of trouble can spread, and I've still some sort of a responsibility here. Anyway, come on in.'

They followed him up the stairway and into the house. It was neat and clean, the floor covered in brightly patterned cotton rugs and the main room furnished with a desk and several deep, old-fashioned leather armchairs. A tiger's head was mounted on a plaque above the empty fireplace.

'Meet Sam,' said North, thumbing toward the trophy. 'The last manager abandoned him.' He waved them into the chairs. 'Well, what's the score? More important, how's Marian?'

'Safe enough.' Cord took one of the cigarettes which North offered. 'Our main worry is whether Nam Ree and his following will decide to take an active hand.'

Prinetti gave a growl. 'More like he would hit a place like this, where the odds would suit him better.'

'Here?' North gave a brief, unimpressed laugh. 'Why? A worn-out mine with a load of rusty equipment. No, I'm more concerned in case some bunch of village hotheads declare open season on outsiders.'

Cord lit his cigarette. 'I almost wish he'd try something,' he said softly. 'I've got three days to find him and get his help to sort out this mess. If I don't, then either we blow up the dam or Myi Teri blows up the tunnel. And he has nine hostages inside it.'

'The thumb-twisting old devil!' North said it with a mixture of surprise and gloomy admiration. 'That really puts you on the spot . . . ' He broke off as the old Pulo woman entered, carrying a tray which was a masterpiece of beaten brassware, and which was incongruously filled by three large breakfast-size china mugs and an old metal coffee pot. She laid the tray down on a small bamboo-legged table and padded out again.

'How about giving me your version of what's happening?' North began pouring the coffee. 'I've only had the army's side, and that's confusing enough.'

Cord told him, sticking to facts and leaving out any mention of suspicions, theories, and his own wider role. When he'd finished, North clasped his arm across his body, pensive.

'Nam Ree might have sent the radio message, I suppose. But I can't see him shooting Myi Teri. It's one thing to prod your friends along into doing what you want, but it's another thing altogether to start shooting them for the same reason.'

'Any better theory on your mind?' Cord looked at him with bland interest.

'We're less than forty miles from the Chinese border,' mused North. 'They've a habit over there of making trouble just for the sheer hell of it. And Nam Ree isn't the only rebel wandering around the hills.'

'Somebody told me that already.' Cord got up, stubbed out his cigarette, and walked over to the small gun rack standing in the far corner of the room. It held a couple of light sporting rifles, with a padlocked chain running through the trigger guards.

'You won't find a .303 there,' said North with a touch of irritation. 'I can manage a .22 using a rest — or a pistol. But that's my limit.'

Prinetti stirred uneasily. 'Maybe I should go out and check over the pick-up, Signor Cord.'

Suddenly North regained his humor. 'Maybe I've a better idea. There couldn't be a nasty idea running in your mind, Cord, that we've maybe hit a new vein of rubies and want to keep the dam from flooding us out?' He chuckled, not waiting for an answer. 'Well, I'll show you. I promised I would anyway, remember?'

He led the way from the house, moving at a brisk pace past the rock garden and out through the rusted machinery and tumble-down huts. At last, he stopped beside one relatively intact mud-brick building, and hammered on the door.

When it opened, a pipestem-thin sallow-skinned man, wearing shorts and a string vest, looked out. 'Tan Das, my foreman,' said North briefly. 'Tan, we're going into the mine. Get a couple of lamps, will you?'

Tan Das rubbed a hand over his sparse, straggling hair and smiled, showing a mouthful of twisted, overlapping teeth. Then he disappeared back into the hut, closing the door.

'Like to know my total payroll?' said North. 'I've got Tan, a couple of other men, and old Gina up at the house. The rest have gone back to their villages.'

'Where's he from?' asked Cord, nodding toward the closed door.

'Rangoon, he says.' North wrinkled his nose expressively. 'I've a feeling he got out for a reason. But he's been with me two years and he makes a good foreman — ask Prinetti.'

The Italian nodded. 'Twice I offer him a job at the dam, twice he says no.'

The hut door opened again and Tan Das came out. He had pulled an old woolen sweater over his vest and he carried an electric storm lantern in each hand. Cord took stock of the man's build and face. Part Chinese, part coast Burmese, he guessed; there were plenty like him along the Rangoon water-front.

'I think maybe I stay out here and have a smoke,' Prinetti decided. 'I've been through the place before. *Permette?*'

'Suit yourself,' agreed North. 'Ready, Cord?'

He nodded, and North led the way,

Tan Das following a pace or two behind them. They headed straight for the rock face, then turned into the angled gash of a narrow ravine. At its end was the start of the mine, the mouth of a low but wide cave which had been strongly buttressed by wooden roof props. Electric wiring led along the rock, but the big fuse box just inside the cave mouth hung open, its circuits broken.

'Watch your head,' warned North, taking one of the lamps. They went into a damp, sewer-like world, where the air was stale and white fungus growths thrived unhindered. North's voice echoed as they walked. 'Don't ask me how long this place has been worked. The company took over the concession about forty years back, made a nice steady profit, too, until they had to get out before the Japs arrived.'

'Were you here before the war?' Cord trod on something soft and wriggling and felt it squelch beneath his shoe.

'No. I was a forestry man. But losing a wing didn't help in that line. I packed it in a few years ago and got this job.'

North stopped and held the lamp high above his head.

Tan Das came forward and the two lamps shone into a vast, domed cavern. Water dripped somewhere in the impenetrable darkness beyond.

'The stuff they dug out of here netted a fortune,' said North, swinging his light beam around. 'But that was before my time, long before it.'

They moved on. A cluster of pin-bright eyes reflected down from one section of the roof; bats had found a happy home in the Ronul workings.

On the far side of the cavern North halted again at the start of three obviously man-made galleries. He shone his lamp briefly into the left-hand section. It ended after some twelve feet against a face of dark, raw granite. 'A bad bet,' he said tersely.

Then, head bent low, he led the way into the middle gallery, past a rack of kerosene emergency lanterns. Halfway along its length the walls showed a gradual change in structure. Bands of solid, hewn granite, still showing the marks of picks and drills, grew more and more frequent between the softer lines of the limestone seam. Now and again a short side gallery led off the main one, where a potential seam had been exploited.

It took five minutes to reach the end of the gallery, a blunt, hammerhead bulge where the air was foul. A broken shovel lay on the floor, covered with a fine layer of undisturbed dust. North held the lamp against the unbroken face of granite rock.

'See these holes? We drilled through and kept on drilling. But the limestone fault ends here,' North said.

'You called it a freak last night,' Cord mused.

'A freak,' North agreed. 'If the seam continues, then it could be half a mile down and a hundred miles away, for all we know.'

'What about the other gallery?' Cord shivered in spite of himself. The atmosphere was as chill as it was dank and foul.

'Number three?' North nodded to his

foreman. 'He wants the full treatment, Tan.'

The crooked teeth flashed a protest. 'It is not safe, Mr. North. The roof . . . '

'Let him see it,' grunted North, a slight edge to his voice. 'If the roof falls, we're still insured — I think.'

Tan Das scowled, but led the way back to the cavern. North waited until Cord emerged, then shone his lamp on the last of the galleries. 'Welcome to North's folly.' He grimaced. 'This is where we finally dried up, on stockholders' patience as well as stones.'

The gallery was obviously newer than the others. Its roof props and wedges had a fresh, clean appearance, and the electric cable running along its walls might have been put up only days before. It had adequate headroom and ran arrow straight. As they went in, a rat suddenly blinked in one of the lamp beams, then scurried away from them and disappeared.

'What went wrong?' asked Cord.

'Nothing — at first. We hit two good pockets of crystalline limestone, even found a handful of seven-carat stones. I got a bonus for them. Then,' North shone the lamp forward. The gallery ended in a tangled mass of fallen rock, broken roof props, and twisted cable. 'The whole damned Ridge fell in on us, that's what happened. There's another fifty feet of gallery from there on — and five bodies. We couldn't get them out.'

Cord thought of the rat and knew a flicker of nausea.

'And you've never tried to re-open it?'

'We hadn't the money or the prospects.' North shook his head. 'All this was eighteen months ago, just before the dam project started. Being told we'd be flooded out was a blessing, even without this cave-in. We'd gone thirty feet without hitting limestone. Anyway, look at the roof . . . ' It was a nightmare of wide, interlaced cracks. One giant slab hung loose, poised as if ready to fall then and there. 'No, we ran out of luck, that's all. It happens.'

Cord nodded. Ronul was a derelict, a snuffed out gamble — that was beyond question. He stepped closer to the debris, one hand resting lightly on the nearest of the surviving roof props, seeing the way in which the great slabs of granite had crushed down on wood and wire. The men beneath it would have known only a second of agony.

A strip of webbing protruded from beneath one sharp-edged block, which could have weighed close to half a ton. Cord bent lower, peering at the webbing in the dim light. Once it had been a sling for a water bottle — the bottle's neck, flattened, was just visible. He glanced around, peered at the webbing again, then turned, beckoning Tan Das nearer.

'Mind if I use that lamp a moment?'

'Be careful . . . ' The man came warily forward, eying the roof, holding the lamp forward at the limit of his reach. Then, with inches to go, he stumbled and overbalanced.

Helpless to intervene, Cord saw the pipestem figure collide solidly with North, hitting him on his unprotected left side, then clutching wildly at the mine manager as they fell together. Both lamps hit the rock floor in a tinkling of broken glass, and the shock of sudden, utter darkness was doubled and redoubled by a louder crackle of freeing wood. The heavy length of roof prop came crashing down, brushing Cord's shoulder on its way to hit the gallery floor. Marooned and lost in an unrelieved blackness he could almost feel, Cord heard a new sound, heart-stopping in its menace, a creak of moving rock overhead, a grinding, grumbling shifting which grew in intensity.

'Get out.' North's shout from somewhere near was frantic in its urgency. 'Get out — it's starting.'

Cord began to obey — and ran straight into the solid rock of the tunnel wall, all sense of direction lost. Small stones were pattering down, and fresh grit was in the air sucking into his lungs.

'Cord . . . '

The grinding grew louder, then just as suddenly ceased. A bright spark flashed for a heartbeat of time, and Cord catapulted himself in its direction. Behind him came a noise like the end of the world, and then North's cigarette lighter had flickered to life and they were hurrying back along the gallery, guided by its fluttering flame. The thunder behind them ceased and gave way to a gentle, almost mewing sound of creaking.

North slowed, gulping for breath. 'That's it — for now.'

He turned and held the lighter high, and both men swallowed as they saw where they'd been standing, a place now solidly packed from floor to roof with a jagged wall of fallen rock.

'Where's Tan?' For the first time in the seconds since the cave-in had begun, Cord thought of the twisted-toothed foreman.

'He got out,' North grunted. 'I don't blame him for that. But the ruddy fool could have killed us.'

'I was the one who asked for the lamp . . . ' Cord followed the mine manager back along the gallery, using his own cigarette lighter to supplement North's fading flame.

Two-thirds of the way back along the gallery Tan Das reappeared, coming toward them waving one of the kerosene emergency lanterns. He bounded the last few yards toward them with a flood of apologies.

'*Ma kaung* — it was bad. If I had not slipped like a *mye* . . . '

'You did,' said North bluntly. 'Stop weeping about it and let's get out of here.'

They headed back in single file, Cord coming last and moving with a new ice-cold caution which cloaked a throbbing anger.

Tan Das's fall and its consequences had had all the hall-marks of accident, except for one thing — the reason why he'd made such a show of wanting more light to look at that webbing sling. The sling hadn't interested him. What had was the glimpse he'd gotten of the roof prop beside him, a thick, sturdy four-by-four but with an angled saw cut running across it near to the base. It was a line which had once been camouflaged by grease that matched the color of the wood — but rats ate grease.

Ronul might be derelict, yet someone had gone to a lot of time and trouble to arrange that booby trap. Sawn almost through and at just the right angle, the roof prop had been calculated to give under any heavy blow.

It had — and had almost taken him with it, but for North and the sparking flint in his cigarette lighter. Which left Tan Das. Had he rigged the trap? Whatever the evidence, it was lost and buried under the fallen rock.

Prinetti was waiting at the tunnel mouth, and a cloud of anxiety lifted from his face as they emerged. 'I was jus' ready to come in after you,' he declared. 'I heard what sounded like trouble.'

'Another rock fall,' said Cord. He forced a grin. 'After that, we called it a day.'

'My fault, Mr. Cord.' Tan Das blinked in the daylight. 'I can only make humble apology for my carelessness.' He scuffed his feet on the ground and glanced toward North. 'I will have new shoring put in there this afternoon, to prevent any spread.'

'Why bother?' The mine manager shook his head. 'The whole damn place can fall down as far as I'm concerned, just as long as I'm not underneath it. Leave it.'

The man nodded, made a short bobbing bow toward them, and went away.

'Prinetti!' Cord caught the bearded Italian's eye. 'We'll be heading back soon. You said you wanted to give the pick-up a check, didn't you? She should be all right, but . . . '

'I'll make sure.' Prinetti gave a large, open wink and headed off on his errand.

'I've heard cleverer ways of telling someone to fade from the scene,' mused North. 'Still, it served. But why?'

Cord strolled on with him, then stopped beside the rusted cylindrical bulk of an old steam boiler. 'Marian gave me a message for you. Want to hear it?'

'Naturally.' North pulled out his cigarette case, shrugged when Cord shook his head, and put the case away again, unopened.

'She said she hoped you'd help, even though she's staying.' Cord leaned back against the boiler casing, watching the mine manager's face tighten. 'That seems to mean something to you.'

North nodded. 'Lets me know this is important to her. I wanted Marian to leave with me when the mine floods. She said no — and was probably right.' He glanced down toward his empty sleeve. 'There's this for a start, and a twenty-year-age gap. Anyway, that's past.' He turned his attention squarely on Cord. 'What do you want? Straight out, no sparring around — even Prinetti can't take all day mooning around that truck.'

'I want to meet Nam Ree. Tonight, if possible.'

'Just like that?' The mine manager's tone was quizzical. 'Why come to me?'

'Because of a story that you have a business arrangement with him — or had.'

'That's an old one.' North raised a frosty twinkle. 'Tell me something, Cord. Whose side are you on?'

'Side?' Cord shook his head. 'Nobody's side. I just want to stop trouble.'

'Maybe there's more trouble than you

think, including the political kind.' North pursed his lips. 'Look, I'll tell you this much. The story that I was paying Nam Ree protection money was a blind. He was in the Burma Rifles back in the days when Stilwell was building his Ledo Road, and later, when the Wingate columns were hunting Japs around the hills. Then, just for variety, the Japs began hunting us.' He paused, choosing his words. 'No heroics, Cord. Nobody saved anybody's life, in case that's what you're wondering about. Nam Ree was one of my column officers, that's all. We were on the same side then . . . '

'And you still are?'

'Maybe. One man's bandit is another man's patriot. You should know that, Cord. I'll go this far — none of Nam Ree's men would have shot Myi Teri. I know Nam Ree didn't. Is that clear enough?'

Cord nodded. An entirely new possibility was gradually emerging — and if anything, he liked it less than the original. 'I still want to see him.'

'On his terms?'

'Any way he wants, as long as it gives me the slightest chance of persuading him to help.' Cord spoke with a desperate sense of purpose. 'You're my only chance now, North, maybe the Pulo's only chance, too. You know what would happen if these hostages died. The Pulos would be hunted all over these hills.'

'Maybe there's more going on than you realize,' said North softly. 'Maybe Nam Ree's got too much at stake.'

Cord gave a slow nod of agreement. 'That's possible. But I still want the chance to talk to him.'

North sighed. 'Let's say I'll contact him. If he says yes, then he'll have his own way of letting you know.'

'Fine.' Cord held out his hand to seal the bargain.

North gripped it wryly, then stayed where he was while Cord began to walk toward the pick-up.

'North,' Cord spun around, 'I meant to ask you. Was he a good signal officer?'

'The best . . . ' North stopped short, a flicker of annoyance on his face. Then he laughed. He was still there, still shaking his head, as the Renault drove away.

* * *

They got back to the Thamaung camp at a little after two P.M. Cord parked the Renault beside the project office and climbed out, hungry but with a glimmer of hope. Even the sight of Captain Paya striding toward him couldn't dull his mood.

'How 'bout eating with us, Signor Cord?' asked Prinetti, closing the passenger door with an affectionate slap of one ham-like hand. 'Anna would like it.'

'And so would I,' agreed Cord. 'Unless the army has any objections.' He greeted Paya with a nod. 'I've got one piece of news for you, Captain. Nam Ree was a signal officer.'

The soldier brushed that aside. 'At the moment there is a more immediate matter, Mr. Cord, much more immediate.' The sheer disciplined restraint in his voice was more effective than anything else short of hysteria. 'I would suggest you have sandwiches and coffee. The radioman Donaldson has been murdered, and I have ordered Miss Frey to be held under house arrest until a proper inquiry has been carried out.'

4

Andy Donaldson's body lay sprawled face down on the floor between the bed and a small desk in his room in the main staff block. An overturned chair and the way he'd fallen showed he'd been sitting at the desk when his attacker had struck — and the army bayonet in his back left only a short length of blade visible below the hilt.

'That's how he was found less than an hour ago. Nothing has been moved, I saw to that.' Captain Paya leaned dolefully against a small dressing table while Cord knelt to examine the thin, slight figure. The Scot's right arm was folded beneath him, the left was extended, the hand bent like a claw against one desk leg. It was as if its action had been frozen while the man had been making a final, unavailing attempt to drag himself upright.

Cord took his time, noting the slow seepage of blood which had soaked through Donaldson's cotton work jacket, spreading itself out from the bayonet wound. An uncapped fountain pen had rolled part way under the desk. Its nib had been twisted by the fall. He raised the dead man gently, saw the blood froth dried around his lips, the stain of blue ink on the index finger of the right hand, then lowered the body back to its original position.

He rose up, grim-faced. 'And Marian Frey?'

'Miss Frey was found by one of my officers.' Captain Paya's manner was one of reluctant distaste. 'She was in this room and apparently searching the top of this desk. Donaldson was there on the floor, and was still not quite dead. He attempted to speak, but . . . ' The soldier shrugged. 'The problem now is surely what we should do. In other places one could lift a telephone, the civil police would arrive, and their fingerprint experts and technicians would begin work. But here? The nearest policeman with any of these skills is a considerable distance away, Mr. Cord. I suggest we must presume to begin our own investigation; Dr. Holst has already examined the body.'

Cord had to agree. Murder might change many things, and outside agencies would be involved, whether he liked it or not. But for the moment, he and Paya were on their own. He walked over to the window and looked out. The staff block, a long single-story prefabricated bungalow, sat about twenty yards away from the main project office. Donaldson's room, a fifteen-foot square box with a built-in cupboard in one corner, was the last of four rooms in the block's length, connected by an outside corridor with the block's entrance door at the far end.

'Suppose we start with the man who found Miss Frey here.' Cord lit a cigarette and watched the smoke drift from its tip. 'Better get Holst and Marian Frey over, too. Anyone else directly involved?'

'So far, no.' Paya crossed to the room door and opened it. Outside, a soldier sentry snapped to attention. Paya gave the man a series of low-voiced instructions, then closed the door again.

Cord moved around the corpse on the floor and inspected the desk top. A slide rule, some magazines, and an old tumbler filled with pencils and ballpoint pens were placed neatly to one side. A blotter lay at an angle, papers and a tumbled desk calendar scattered over it. In the far corner a small, cheap clock ticked away the time. Cord thumbed through the papers; they were routine technical memos. 'Where'd the bayonet come from? One of yours?'

'It was taken from the police post last night.' Paya brushed the embarrassment aside. 'There is a fairly simple explanation — Dr. Holst knows the background of it.'

A knock on the door and its opening stopped Cord from asking for more. The young army officer who entered was slim, with a pencil-line mustache. He gave a slightly nervous salute and eyed them warily.

Paya returned the salute in a weary reflex. 'Lieutenant Maung,' he said briefly. Then, for his junior's benefit, 'Mr. Cord is the senior United Nations representative present. Tell him what you know, briefly, Maung. And relax. This is neither the parade ground nor a court martial.'

The youngster moistened his lips. 'When I opened the door and came into this room, sir, the man was lying on the floor as he is. Miss Frey was standing over him and seemed to be looking for something on his desk. I — I went around and bent over the man. He was still alive, and his eyes were open.'

'You spoke to him?' asked Cord.

Lieutenant Maung nodded. 'I spoke loudly, with my lips close to his ear. I asked him who had stabbed him, but,' his face twisted briefly at the memory, 'he just looked at me, made a noise, and — and died.'

'And died,' echoed Paya. 'You then spoke to Miss Frey. Correct?'

'Yes, sir.' Maung's eyes strayed over to the partly visible figure lying behind the desk. 'I asked her why she had done it.'

'The direct approach.' A wisp of a smile appeared on Paya's broad, unemotional face. '*Kaung bey* — go on.'

'She said that she too had just arrived and found him.' The young soldier shrugged. 'I went to the window and looked out. Some of the camp workmen were playing dice outside the block and I opened the window and shouted to them. *Ma we bu* — it is not far away. Then I waited with Miss Frey until help arrived. When it did, I posted a sentry outside this door and took Miss Frey with me to report to you, sir.'

Cord looked at Paya and received a brief, confirming nod.

'I was using one of the offices over in the administration building,' Paya grunted. 'I told Maung to stay with the girl, came over here to see for myself, then arranged for her to be held in her quarters.'

'Was she searched?'

'By Mrs. Prinetti and Miss Marsh, at my request — in privacy, of course.' Paya showed the untarnished pride of a man who considered he'd been meticulous in attention to detail. 'They found certain notes in her shirt pocket relating to Donaldson.'

'I asked her for them,' said Cord shortly. 'All right, let's go back to the beginning. Lieutenant, why did you come to Donaldson's room?'

Lieutenant Maung cleared his throat uneasily. 'To — to ask him to give me back our bayonet,' he said awkwardly. 'Dr. Holst had told me it was here. Donaldson used it last night to cut loose the men who were left bound at the police post, and had kept it.'

'No other bayonets missing?'

Maung shook his head. 'Just rifles, Mr. Cord.'

The Pulos had their *dahs* — and by comparison the bayonets would have been dismissed as toys. Cord looked around for an ash tray, saw none, and stubbed his cigarette out underfoot.

'Did you see Miss Frey entering the staff block?'

This time the Lieutenant nodded. 'I was still talking to Dr. Holst. We were not far away, and we both noticed her go in. It would be three, perhaps four minutes before I followed.'

'Anyone else come or go during that time?'

'No, sir.' Maung was stiffly positive. 'And I was with the Doctor for some minutes beforehand. I would have noticed any earlier arrivals or departures.'

'Then, when you found her here, did you ask what she was looking for on the desk?' asked Cord.

The young soldier hesitated, then shook his head. 'No. The first thing I wanted to do was to get help.'

Cord sighed. 'All right, Lieutenant, but imagine there was someone else in this room before Miss Frey arrived. Couldn't he have heard her coming and gotten out of that window? That's how Donaldson escaped from here when the Pulos raided. It's at the back of the block, out of sight from where you were standing.'

'I'll answer that.' Paya sucked his lips unhappily. 'The point occurred to me, Mr. Cord, but I spoke to the dice players. They were only feet away from that window. No one could have come out without their knowing. There is a reason why I believe them — raise the window for yourself.'

Cord crossed over, gripped the bottom sash by its handles, and pulled. It rose with a squeal of ill-fitting wood. The window might have served Andy Donaldson as a hurried escape route, but . . .

'At such a short distance, and with such noise, it would be impossible,' shrugged Paya. He turned to his subordinate. 'All right, we will see Dr. Holst next.'

Lieutenant Maung saluted and went out, leaving the door ajar. Almost immediately Dr. Holst pushed it open again and stumped in, his whole manner one of bristling aggression. 'Well, what's the idea this time?' he demanded. 'Look, Paya, I don't mind you playing at policeman, but . . . ' He broke off as he saw Cord. 'You're back, eh? Well, maybe you can tell the gallant Captain where he gets off. Marian use that bayonet?' He gave a derisive sniff at the idea.

'All we are doing is conducting a preliminary inquiry,' soothed Paya, going over and closing the door. 'It was Mr.

Cord's suggestion that you should be here.'

'Hmm.' Dr. Holst swung his glare toward Cord. 'And were you also the reason why Marian was down at the drivers' billets this morning asking about the man I'd treated?'

'Just a matter of being sure where I stood,' murmured Cord.

Paya showed his annoyance. 'I knew nothing of this!'

'And Andy Donaldson was probably another on her list, eh?' the Doctor went on, completely ignoring the soldier. 'Well, now, couldn't that make you directly responsible for the mess she's in?'

'I've thought of that,' agreed Cord with a bitterness which stopped Holst from continuing his rumblings.

'Where do we start? Cause of death?' He became strictly professional.

Cord nodded. 'And what you know about the bayonet.'

'Right. The wound first. The bayonet was used at a downward angle, probably by someone standing over him. I was asked to leave it in the wound, which means I haven't made a full examination. But the blade went in just to the right of the vertebral column and over the eighth interspace. Allowing the angle and the normal length of these damned tin-openers, that gives a penetration of about four inches. At a guess,' he snorted and glanced at Paya, 'at a guess I'd say it penetrated the basal lobe of the right lung. Cause of death would be massive hemorrhaging. It was a pretty powerful blow, maybe two-handed.'

'Yet he didn't die right away,' Cord reminded him.

'Why should he?' Holst sighed at the need for explanation. 'A bayonet makes a penetrating wound, with not much surface blood. Inside the lung bleeding isn't something you can time with a stopwatch. Five minutes, even at the outside ten minutes of life would be quite possible.' He crossed the room and looked down at the body. 'The bayonet now, that's quite simple. I saw Donaldson just before lunch. We were talking about last night, and he remembered the thing was still lying in his room. He said he'd be working here for a spell, but would hand it back to the military later. I just happened to mention the fact to Lieutenant Maung.'

'You said a powerful blow,' said Paya suddenly, piecing the theory into his own pattern. 'And perhaps two-handed — would that not point to a woman, conscious of her lack of strength?'

'Ever tried to bury a knife in someone's back?' asked the Doctor coldly. 'If you had, Captain, you'd be surprised at the effort it takes, even for a full-grown man.' He prodded the body gently with the toe of one dust-covered shoe. 'How long do you propose to — ah — leave things as they are? It's a warm afternoon.'

Captain Paya scratched his chin, anxious as ever to do the right thing. 'We should have some record of how he was found. The authorities will require it.'

'They might not be here for some time,' said Holst dryly. 'I can bring a camera and take some photographs.'

The army man accepted the offer with open relief.

'Anyone had a look through his

pockets yet?' asked Cord. He took his answer from their silence, knelt down, and made a swift check. Donaldson's personal possessions seemed scanty, a thin wallet with a few kyat notes, a package of chewing gum, an old penknife, and a crumpled handkerchief. 'Doctor, how well did you know him?'

'Young Donaldson?' Holst shrugged. 'A quiet fellow, competent, friendly enough, interest in local customs and dialects — that sort of thing. He saw me professionally a couple of times, complaining of headache and eyestrain, but there's not much more I can tell you. Lona Marsh was closest to him, no doubt of that.'

'You've seen her since this happened?'

Holst nodded. 'She's taking it fairly well. So is Marian, come to that, especially when you consider the way she's been treated.' He gave a growl of indignation. 'Hell, she couldn't have done it. She says she didn't, and that's good enough for me.'

'Any blood on her clothing?'

'No. Even if there was, it wouldn't

mean she was guilty,' said Holst, his whole manner growing colder.

'I'm only asking,' said Cord patiently. 'Lieutenant Maung says you were with him when Marian went into this block. Did you see anyone else?'

Holst gave a slow, reluctant shake of his head.

'And yet Donaldson must have been stabbed at roughly about the time she entered?'

'Or a minute or two before,' the Doctor qualified the statement determinedly. 'Look, Cord, it's not my job to try to understand what happened. I stick to medical fact. But couldn't one of the Pulos have sneaked back for some reason and done this?' He fidgeted impatiently. 'Well, it is not my job, as I said — if you're finished, I'll go and get that camera.'

Cord nodded. 'Right. Marian's outside?'

'Yes. You want her next?'

'Please.' Cord waited until the Doctor had gone out, slamming the door behind him, then turned to Paya. 'You've heard part of this already. I'd asked Marian to gather background for me on the project staff. I asked her about three people in particular — Holst, Donaldson, and Lona Marsh.'

'I see.' The soldier's mouth closed tight for a moment. 'Well, if that is supposed to hold some inner meaning, perhaps it is as well that both Holst and Miss Marsh have alibis — Holst from Lieutenant Maung and the girl from myself. She was working in her office for almost an hour before the murder. I had written a report of events for submission to my headquarters, and she agreed to type a clean copy for me. It runs to several thousand words, Mr. Cord, and she kept working at it throughout the time. The typed version is finished and on my desk at this moment.'

'She didn't leave at all?'

'I can vouch for that — until, of course, she came over here like everyone else to find out what was happening.'

There was a knock on the door, it opened, and Marian Frey was ushered in by the sentry. As the door closed behind her and Cord stepped forward, she looked at him with a flicker of relief. Then, her face pale but determined, she glanced briefly toward the body on the floor.

'Miss Frey,' Paya brought forward a chair in a conscience-saving gesture. 'A cigarette?'

She took it and accepted a light from Cord, still silent, waiting for them to begin.

'Marian, we're running through everyone's story of what happened,' said Cord, trying hard to encourage her with his approach. 'Like to tell your side of it?'

'Is it worth while?' She gave a thin, tight smile, the cigarette burning unheeded between her fingers. 'Captain Paya seems to have heard enough already.'

Paya spread his hands apologetically. 'Believe me, Miss Frey, I like no part of this affair. But the searching, the guard — in the circumstances there are some things I must do.'

'It doesn't matter.' She looked away from them both, toward the window. 'Will this do? I came here to see Andy. I found him lying on the floor, just as he is, and — and he was still alive. I bent down over him and he — he tried to speak to me.' There was effort behind the ragged steadiness of her voice. 'There was blood in his mouth and he was very weak. He could hardly whisper.'

'Could you make any sense out of it?' Cord encouraged her.

She shook her head. 'He said something about his desk, and something else — it sounded like 'notes.' I can't be sure. He was pleading with me . . . ' She bit her lip, then looked straight at him. 'I tried to see if what he wanted was on his desk, and . . . '

'And that was when Lieutenant Maung came in?'

'Yes.' She gave a helpless shrug. 'Maybe it didn't look very pretty, a dying man on the floor and someone standing over him, rifling his desk. But that's what happened.'

Paya gave a nervous cough. 'This business of finding him, Miss Frey, it troubles me. You have witnesses who say you came into this building almost five minutes before Lieutenant Maung followed you. Do you mean you spent all that time with a man dying at your feet and did not think to get help, help which might have saved his life?'

Anger flared in her eyes. 'No, I don't. I didn't come straight here. I made a quick check through the other rooms first.'

Paya grunted. 'Why?'

She glanced at Cord and saw him nod. 'Because Talos had asked me to — to find out what I could about everyone on the project team.'

'I see.' Paya was heavily suspicious. 'But the other three rooms here belong to men who are hostages. You felt it was right to pry through their rooms in this way?'

'She was doing what I asked,' said Cord sharply. 'Any ethics involved are my worry.'

'Very well.' Paya pursed his lips. 'But what brought you to see Donaldson in the first place? Did Mr. Cord also ask you to question his suspects?'

She bit back the anger which flushed her cheeks. 'I looked up the personnel files in Henry Lewis' room this morning.

They showed that Andy had once been a member of a rifle club. I — put off coming here for a time. But then I decided I'd risk it. If Andy was in, I'd just say I'd dropped in for a chat. If he was out . . . '

'Then you'd walk in and look for a rifle?' Paya sighed. 'And did you perhaps find a rifle, Miss Frey? Not here? Not in any of the other rooms?' His voice harshened. 'It comes to this, Miss Frey. You are the only person seen to enter or leave this building. Donaldson dies while you are in this room. Did you kill him?'

Cord put his hand on her shoulder. 'Marian, after you found Andy, did you knock anything off the desk — a fountain pen, for instance?'

Puzzled, she shook her head. 'I was still trying to see what Andy wanted when Lieutenant Maung came in. I'd only a second or two; I hadn't time to touch anything.'

'Look again,' he invited. 'Take your time. Do you see any changes from before?'

She inspected the room with care, then nodded. 'The door of that cupboard was closed.'

'I opened it,' said Paya shortly. 'I am not a policeman, Miss Frey, but the hope did come to me that someone might still have been hiding in there.'

Cord walked over to the cupboard. Its door was flush with the wall, and inside it shelves ran up to the unbroken ceiling. Some held books, others clothing, a few were empty. There was ample free floor space inside it to hold a man, but with that squeaking window and a guard on the door . . . He turned back. 'Marian, could anybody have moved along that corridor while you were checking the other rooms? Could they have slipped past you?'

She moistened her lips. 'I don't know. I don't think so. I heard nothing. When I reached this room I knocked a couple of times and — and then just walked in.' There was an hysterical edge creeping into her voice. 'Shouldn't you take my fingerprints?'

'We could,' he agreed. 'But if there

are prints on that bayonet we can't even start to compare them. That'll have to wait until we bring in someone with the equipment and the know-how.' There was something more important on his mind. 'Paya, why would a man use a fountain pen?'

Paya blinked. '*Ba yaung le* — to write, what else?'

'To write what?' Cord tapped the tumbler filled with pens and pencils. 'These were handy. But a man keeps a fountain pen for special use — writing a check, an important letter, things of that nature. He was using his pen. What for?' He spread out the sheets scattered on the desk. 'Not any of these.'

Paya hurried to the wastepaper basket and found it empty. 'We do not know he had even begun to write,' he objected.

'Look at the index finger of his right hand. Ink-stained — the pen leaked. He was writing, with someone standing behind him.'

'But Miss Frey was searched . . . ' Paya's eyes widened.

'And no letter. Yet she had no chance

to get rid of it,' Cord reminded him. He gave a quick glance of reassurance toward the girl. 'I think it's about time we gave this place a proper going over.'

She waited while they did — every drawer, every shelf in the room. At the end, the entire result was a folder of photographs dating back to Donaldson's native Scotland. Some had been taken at a rifle club meet and one showed Donaldson in a kilt, smiling as he received a trophy.

Cord gnawed his lip for a moment, undecided. 'You knocked on that door then waited. Let's have another look at that cupboard.'

They followed him over, Paya's confidence shaken, a tense hope flushing over Marian's face. Using the shelves as the rungs of a ladder, Cord climbed up, then balanced precariously while he pushed and prodded against the ceiling. They heard him give a thin chuckle of satisfaction.

'Paya, here's your way out.'

He pushed again, using the flat of one hand. The whole ceiling of the cupboard rose and he slid it to one side. Solid from floor-level view, the cupboard's ceiling formed a one-piece service hatch of wood-framed plasterboard, resting snugly against the four walls.

'Simple when you know how . . . ' Cord tested his weight against the shelving, then, in one easy movement, swung himself up and into the dark roof space above. His voice came echoing back to them. 'Stay where you are for a moment.' The hatch slid back into place, and they heard nothing more.

'Miss Frey,' Captain Paya relinquished what little remained of his pride, 'I am embarrassed to the point of pain. Did you know of this hatch?'

She shook her head. 'I wish I had. Much more of what was happening, and you'd have convinced me I was guilty.' A trembling laugh came from her lips. Then, as she saw the alarm spreading over Paya's face, she reassured him. 'No hysterics, Captain, just relief.'

He nodded, led her over to a chair, and made her sit down. She had recovered most of her composure by the time the room door opened and Cord marched in, a slight smear of dust on his grinning face, his hands gripping an empty leather rifle case.

'That's how it was probably done, Paya. Through the ceiling hatch, along the crossbeams above — there's not much space, but there's enough. Each bedroom has a similar hatch, and there's another leading into a broom closet just inside the block entrance. Anyone who knew his way around could have heard Marian knock on the room door and hidden in that cupboard. They may still have been there when Lieutenant Maung arrived and marched her off. But once they got up in the roof space, all they had to do was get down into one of the other cupboards and sneak out as soon as there was a crowd milling around.'

Captain Paya rose above his chagrin. 'And that?' he asked, gesturing toward the rifle case. 'You found it up there?'

Cord nodded. 'There's quite a lot of junk stored in the roof space, but no rifle.'

The leather case was an expensive

hand-tooled job, but dusty from lack of use. Paya took it and sniffed the interior. 'There is still the scent of gun oil, but it is faint.' He glanced at Cord. 'This could be for a .303. You think perhaps part of our motive is here? Perhaps the rifle was taken by the man who shot Myi Teri or . . . ' He left it unfinished, puzzled by the equally vague alternatives. 'Anyway, my apologies again, Miss Frey. All restrictions which were placed on you are removed — at least until more qualified people than myself decide.'

She thanked him with a slight nod of her head. 'I can go?'

'But of course.' Paya bounded to the door, opened it, and beckoned to the sentry. 'The lady is free to do as she wishes.'

Cord tossed the gun case on the bed. 'I'll come along with you, Marian.'

'Wait, Mr. Cord.' Paya shook his head. 'I would prefer if you and I could talk for a moment. Perhaps outside, eh? Dr. Holst will be back soon, and he has work to do here.'

They followed her out of the room.

From a little way along the corridor beyond, Lona Marsh swept toward them in quick, short, determined steps, anger on her face.

'Captain Paya, this idea about Marian, it's nonsense. She couldn't . . . '

Marian Frey caught the raven-haired Anglo-Burmese girl by the arm. 'It's all right, Lona.'

'It isn't,' she insisted. 'They can't . . . '

'Miss Frey is free to do as she wishes,' said Paya wearily. 'Certain new facts have decided this.'

'Oh!' Lona Marsh gave a sigh of satisfaction. 'I could have told you. Anyone who knows Marian could have told you.' She turned to the other girl. 'Let's go then.'

'I'd like a word with you too, Lona,' said Cord. 'You and Andy were close friends. Did he say anything, hint at anything that was worrying him?'

'No. I'd have told Captain Paya if I'd known anything — anything at all.' She bit her lip. 'Marian?'

'In a moment.' She turned toward Cord. 'Talos, I — I owe you quite a lot.'

'Talk about it later,' he advised with a faint grin. 'We've some business left to finish.'

She understood.

* * *

Once they'd quit the staff block, Paya guided Cord in the general direction of the dam. The soldier walked in uneasy silence, but as they cleared the compound area he stopped, thumbs hitched into his webbing belt.

'I believe in being honest about most things, Mr. Cord. I think you should know I sent two signals to Myitkyina before you arrived.' He cleared his throat in an awkward fashion. 'One reported Donaldson's death and asked for civil police assistance.'

'And the other?'

'I reported to headquarters the Pulo ultimatum about the Thamaung — and I asked that a more suitably ranking officer take over this command.'

'You've had replies?'

Paya gritted his teeth. 'Yes. A refusal

to both, Mr. Cord, unless agreed to by you. Also the instruction that I have to — to coöperate with you in any action you consider necessary.' His pride had been badly stung.

'Satisfied with your orders?' asked Cord mildly. 'This co-operation business shouldn't cause any problem.'

'They are orders and I will carry them out,' said Paya with a wooden determination.

They walked on, each with his own thoughts and uncertain of the other's likely response, until they reached the fringes of the dam. The thin line of infantry were still strung out at intervals along the river's edge, but they were men relaxed, moving openly about, tension removed by the knowledge of the necessary truce. Across the dam two Pulo villagers sat equally unconcerned beside the start of the concrete. One had a rifle propped across his knees, both were lazing in the warmth of the sun. Across there, too, still inside the tunnel, were the hostages. Cord shook his head. By their very isolation there was something almost unreal about the men's existence and their plight.

'Too much idleness.' Paya frowned disapprovingly at the scene. 'I think it is time I toured these posts again.'

Cord let him go. An empty feeling in his stomach reminded him it was a long time since he'd last eaten. He headed back to the compound and into the mess hall, then stopped in surprise at the sight of its solitary occupant. Victor Prinetti sat at the left-hand table, busy demolishing a heaped plate of bacon and eggs.

'I thought you were eating at home,' Cord greeted him.

'Huh.' Prinetti shoveled another mouthful home. 'Jus' as well you didn't come with me. Anna looks at me when I come in and says there's been too much excitement for cooking. All she's done is feed the boy and have a sandwich. So I came here.'

The mess boy appeared from the kitchen on quiet, sandaled feet, his face composed in an expression which said clearer than words that late arrivals weren't welcome. It came to Cord being able to choose between the bacon and eggs or an omelette. He chose the latter and ordered a pot of coffee to go with it. By the time the food came, his appetite was honed to a point where he tackled the dish with a gusto almost equal to the Italian's.

Prinetti finished his meal with a sigh and sat back. 'Anna was telling me about Marian Frey — that she had to help to search her. You think she killed Donaldson?'

Cord took a gulp of his coffee and shook his head. 'That's out.' He gave the foreman a brief sketch of what had happened.

'Good.' Prinetti smoothed the ends of his beard with satisfaction. 'She's a damn nice girl, Signor Cord.'

'Did you know Andy Donaldson had a rifle?'

Prinetti grinned. 'I should. I bought it from him.'

'When?' Cord lowered his cup with deliberate care and glared across the table. 'What kind?'

'It was an old British Lee-Enfield

.303.' Prinetti screwed up his eyes in recollection. 'A match weapon, I think he called it. He used to enter shooting competitions until his eyesight began to give out a few years back. I bought it from him 'bout three months back.'

'But not the leather case?'

Prinetti shook his head. 'Couldn't afford it. I'm a family man, remember. Donaldson said he'd keep it and that if I changed my mind then we could talk business again.'

'Why didn't you tell me before?' demanded Cord. 'You knew we were looking for a .303!'

'Because I haven't got it no more,' protested the other man. 'I bought the damn rifle to go hunting. But Anna nagged on about it being a waste of denaro.' He gave a despairing wave of his hands. 'In the end I sold it again.'

'Back to Donaldson?'

'No.' Prinetti gave a wry chuckle. 'I tried, but he wasn't interested. One of our truck men bought it.'

'And he still has it?'

Prinetti rubbed his chin uneasily. 'No,

signor. He sold it outside the camp. I should have remembered this when we were up at the mine, *pero* . . . '

'Who got it?' demanded Cord tensely.

'North's foreman, Tan Das, signor. I would have told you . . . '

'But you didn't.' Cord swore to himself. 'You know the reason for that rock fall at the mine today? It happened because somebody had pretty well sawed through a roof prop — and Tan Das happened to knock it down when I was on the wrong side of it.'

'Signor, I am sorry.' Prinetti gave an unhappy rumble. 'Look, suppose I go back up to the mine, take this *gallo* Tan Das, and knock his head against a rock until he tells me what he knows?'

'Not yet.' Cord shook his head. 'But if I need help, I'll tell you.'

From the mess hall Cord headed back to his guest hut. Once inside, he threw his jacket over a chair, peeled off his shirt, and ran water from the tap to fill the tiny washbasin. He reached for the rough-cut block of green household soap, dipped it in the water, then stopped. A wedge of white paper was lying in the soap dish. Cord grabbed and unfolded it without taking time to dry his hands.

The writing was in bold, exact capitals: ACROSS THAMAUNG FORD AT NINE TONIGHT. MR. NORTH'S FRIEND WILL BE NEAR.

Half an hour later Cord set out again. The first and completely unproductive stop was at the radio shack. There were ample signs that Andy Donaldson had begun an attempt to clear up the wreckage and repair what damage he could. But, though he took time over it, Cord could find no hint or trace of anything which might have had any bearing on the radioman's murder.

At last he gave up and set out to locate Marian. His first try was at the project office block, where the fast tapping of a typewriter guided him along the corridor to Lona Marsh's office. She was busy, her fingers rippling over the keyboard of her machine with a mechanical ease; and he'd been standing in the doorway for almost a minute before she realized he was there. She gave him a friendly enough nod and stopped typing at the end of a line.

'Can I help you, Mr. Cord?'

'I don't know yet.' He came across the room and perched on the edge of her desk. 'Cigarette?'

'Thanks.' She took one between small, neat fingers which had the nails trimmed short and polished pearl pink. He lit the cigarette, took one for himself, and glanced down at the machine.

'Still finding work?'

'This?' she shrugged. 'Just something to do, records I've been meaning to tidy up for months. It takes my mind off other things.'

'Things like Andy Donaldson's death?' It was the first time they'd talked alone, and he inspected her with open deliberation. She was like a plump, attractive kitten in build; but the bright dark eyes told a different story, held a quality of strength striking in contrast.

She took the inspection coolly. 'Andy's death for one, Mr. Cord. I liked him, I liked him a lot. Right now I'm glad it didn't go beyond liking. It's bad enough this way, that he's dead and we don't know who killed him.' The fingers of her right hand toyed absently with the typewriter's keys. 'Then there's Mr. Lewis and the others. What's going to happen there?'

'What makes you think the answer depends on me?'

'Doesn't it?' She leaned back, an action which put a gentle curving strain against her nylon blouse, and gave a faint smile. 'I think most things are up to you now.'

'Maybe.' He sensed an underlying interrogation in her voice and deliberately gave her a morsel to consider. 'The dam stays, Lona.'

'Then what else can you do?' she demanded. 'Even a miracle worker would find it hard to persuade the Pulos to go back as things stand.'

'Maybe I know somebody who can do just that.' He saw the flicker of keen interest which crossed her face, but left it at that. 'Any idea where I'll find Marian?'

'Try the village.' She seemed to lose

interest in him. The typewriter's carriage swung back to begin a new line, and he left as her fingers began their lightning tattoo again.

* * *

Marian was at the far side of the Pulo village when Cord first spotted her. She was standing beside one of the thatched stilt houses, talking to two small, wrinkle-faced native women. One of them saw him coming and let out a quick, shrill cry. Next moment, both women had picked up the wrapped bundles lying at their feet, had the bundles on their backs and the supporting headbands on their foreheads, and were scurrying off toward the rank growth of tall grass and prickly shrubs which fringed the trees.

Cord came on without changing his pace. He had an idea more than one pair of eyes were watching him from the forest edge.

'Did I break up something?'

'In a way.' Marian was vaguely exasperated despite the warmth of her greeting. 'I thought some of the women would slip back to collect things they needed. I was lucky. I met two I knew.'

'How are they managing?'

'All right so far. Most of them are with relatives further up the valley. A few of the women who don't have young children to worry about are sticking fairly close to home.' She became more serious. 'Talos, I was — well — I was worried stiff for a spell this afternoon. Finding Andy like that was enough of its own. But what came after . . . '

'It's over now. The best thing's to forget about it.'

'I want to,' she said feelingly.

'Right. Then let's talk about what you found out earlier.' He jerked her mind away from the memory.

'There isn't much. Dr. Holst's call to a patient was absolutely genuine, the man still has a raging fever. Lona looked in on the Prinettis on the way home from the radio hut and — well — I told you about Andy being a keen rifleman.'

'He used to be. We've got a possible

lead on who has his rifle now.' He didn't bother to explain. 'What about backgrounds?'

'Dr. Holst has been on U.N. postings for eight years and came here when the project began. Two months ago he asked for a transfer; he found the place too quiet. It was refused. Andy — well there's really nothing much. He was at sea for a spell as a radio operator before he came here. About the only other thing is that he had an appointment to see Henry Lewis today. I don't know why and neither does Lona.'

'And Lona?' He raised a questioning eyebrow.

'Well . . . ' There was the same reluctance as before. 'I found her file card. Lewis' previous secretary resigned just over a year ago because of family illness. Lona had been working in an office in Myitkyina; she got this job on the recommendation of some friend at the U.N. mission staff at Rangoon.'

'And the rest?' They had been walking slowly as they talked. Now they stopped beside a broad-spread carpet of blue trumpet-flowered gentians. The buzz of insects filled the scented, sun-warmed air.

'I got a little on everyone.' She unfastened the breast pocket of her blouse and took out a folded wad of close-written notes. 'Sorry I don't type.'

He glanced at the top page. The handwriting was small and neat.

She watched him, her fingers toying with the shirt button. 'What happened when you saw Maurice?'

'He's done what I wanted.'

'Then you're really making progress!'

He nodded. Events were starting to move, but whether the result would sweep him into more of a mess or land him on the path toward daylight, he still didn't care to guess.

She took a step closer to him, still fumbling with the pocket button. 'Talos, I like to pay my debts.'

He forgot the eyes in the trees, took her into his arms, and helped her make sure she did. If there had ever been a hint of ice about the slim, gray-eyed brunette, it had long since melted from her lips . . .

* * *

At five, Cord was back at the guest hut. Minutes later Captain Paya arrived, sat down, and smoked the first of a chain of cigarettes, while he told Cord the result of Dr. Holst's post-mortem. The cause of death had been as the Doctor had suggested, a deep penetrating wound into the lower lobe of the right lung. Donaldson could have lived those vital extra minutes. There had been another message from Myitkyina; the soldier groaned at the memory.

'They want hourly reports — hourly! What am I supposed to tell them? That — that you have been spending an enjoyable afternoon among the flowers with a lady only theoretically cleared of suspicion of murder?'

'Well, now!' Cord was mildly reproachful. 'Who's been keeping an eye on me?'

'Not on you,' said Paya stiffly. 'On Miss Frey. I assigned Lieutenant Maung to the task. He felt somewhat embarrassed.'

'He could have turned away.' Cord chuckled. 'Well, you can tell them that a new possibility of negotiation is opening.'

'There is?' Paya's head jerked up. 'How?'

'Supposing you just agree that you leave a jeep parked out of sight in a quiet path of the village — and that you make sure no one notices when I drive it out of camp this evening.'

The soldier's mouth closed like a trap. 'Out of camp . . . '

'And nobody following,' said Cord. 'I mean it. If anyone gets too curious, tell them I'm tired and went to bed early — anything you like. I'll leave my pick-up lying outside the administration office to lend a bit of color to the story.'

'I see.' Paya took a long, serious draw on his current cigarette. 'I think — I think I would rather not be told who you go to meet. But I can guess. You have some means of defense if things go wrong?'

'If I had, I'd be a fool to take it with me.'

'You take one weapon,' sighed Paya. 'Your tongue, Mr. Cord. It has a certain gift for charming birds from the trees. I once knew another man with this same gift. He was Irish — a strange race. You are not Irish, Mr. Cord, at least, I do not think so.'

'Sorry to disappoint you,' Cord chuckled. 'Still, I'll do the best I can.'

'I wish you luck.' Captain Paya made it sound a gloomy benediction.

* * *

At exactly eight by the hands of his wrist watch, Cord made his way out of the night-darkened compound and, keeping well into the shadows, went across to the silent huts of the Pulo village. The jeep was there as he'd been promised. He started it, drove quietly up the tree-lined hill track, and then settled down to the journey ahead.

It was the same rough, bouncing route as before. Occasionally a pair of animal eyes would glint back from the lancing beam of his headlights along the roadside scrub. That apart, Cord might have been alone in the world, as the sturdy little vehicle throbbed on. He reached the ford, splashed the jeep across it, then stopped on dry ground at the other side; switched on his lights, left the driver's seat, and waited patiently, leaning back against the comfortable warmth of the radiator.

Time passed. The cloud-covered moon gave him only an occasional glimpse of the rippling water, and what lay beyond in any direction remained a dark, shapeless shadow. The only sounds above the low, steady noise of the water were the occasional splash of a small fish and, from the distance, the occasional screech of a tree owl. It was a nerve-lulling atmosphere. On his second cigarette, still resting against the jeep, he felt an almost electric shock when something hard and round prodded firmly against his back.

He stayed where he was, his hands openly in view. There was an immediate rustle of footsteps and two men appeared out of the darkness, each cradling a short, stubby automatic rifle. The pressure on his back eased an instant later, and their companion came around to join them.

'From Nam Ree?' asked Cord.

The trio's faces, dark etchings in the

filtered moonlight, remained expressionless. One man stepped forward and ran his hands in a rapid search over Cord's clothing. Another got aboard the jeep and did a similar job in a minimum of time and little noise. Now that they were closer, Cord could see more of them. They were dressed alike, in rough, handwoven shirts and pantaloons. *Dah* knives hung from the army issue webbing belts around their waists, and their feet were snug in leather sandals.

A satisfied growl came from the jeep. The nearest of the two men with Cord raised a hand in acknowledgment, then said awkwardly, '*Kaung ba-byi* — it is good. Please you will drive.'

Cord nodded. They climbed aboard with him, one in front, the other two behind. He started the engine, but as the lights were switched on, a rough hand gripped his arm and the Pulo beside him shook his head.

'All right.' Cord grimaced, snapped the lights off again, put the jeep into gear, and set off at a crawl. As a journey it was a slow, jolting nightmare, but his passengers seemed able to both sense and see every inch of what lay ahead. They guided him with a tap on the shoulder and a finger pointed either to right or left. Then, gradually, they relaxed. His passenger-seat navigator produced a handful of cheroots and offered one to Cord with what approached a friendly grunt, then struck a kitchen match on the sole of his sandal to light up.

The journey continued, and their route began to climb up from the valley floor. The moonlight gave Cord fleeting impressions of fantasy shapes of rock and grotesquely twisted trees. He felt the palms of his hands grow damp with perspiration, and more than once lifted them from the steering wheel to wipe them surreptitiously on the legs of his slacks.

The track they traveled seemed to wind back on itself at places. More than once Cord became conscious he was crawling along close to a precipice edge, and felt thankful that its full terror was hidden by the night. But at last his navigator gave a nod of satisfaction and signaled him to stop. They got out, one man staying near the jeep while the other two led Cord in a scrambling ascent of the hillside, traveling over loose rock and rustling, knife-edged grass.

'Wait.' His navigator halted, gasped for breath for a moment, then put his fingers to his mouth and gave a short, sharp whistle. It was answered from a little way ahead, and the Pulo gestured that Cord should go on alone. He struggled on about another twenty feet up the sharp, unfamiliar slope, stopped again to take his bearings, and heard a soft, rumbling laugh.

'Over here, Mr. Cord,' said a rich, deep, vastly amused voice. 'At the risk of sounding theatrical, welcome to the Cave of Bats.'

5

The same rich, deep chuckle as before came from the darkness, while Talos Cord tried to locate its source. There was a rustle of canvas and a shielded beam of yellow light shone from a narrow crack in the rocks about ten yards away. The man who stood framed in the glow beckoned him forward.

'Welcome, Mr. Cord — and forgive the precautions.' Nam Ree waited until Cord had joined him, then pulled the canvas back in place, shutting out the night. 'Though my men would make very sure you were not followed, there is always the problem of an inquisitive army patrol. Besides, I would prefer it if you were unlikely to find your way back to this *ku*.' The Pulo rebel's exacting, almost pedantic style reflected his school-teaching past.

'You did a good job on all counts.' Cord looked around him, frankly curious.

The light came from a trimmed, shaded oil lamp, and the crack in the rocks was in reality the start of a low, narrow cave extending back into the hill. 'I've no complaints.'

Nam Ree seemed both amused and pleased. 'If we go on a little way, we will be considerably more comfortable.' He picked up the lamp, brightened its flame, and led the way. Cord followed his example, stooping to avoid his head banging against the roof. After only a short distance Nam Ree stopped, stretched to his full height, and raised the lamp above his head. The cave's tunnel widened into a pocket, which had the dimensions of a small room, then continued on as before. Blankets had been spread in one corner and a woven reed basket lay beside these.

'In a moment we can talk.' Nam Ree placed the lamp on a niche of rock, then went over and sat in cross-legged ease on the rough couch, nodding approvingly as Cord followed his example. Nam Ree wore much the same clothes as his followers, but with a holstered automatic at his waist and a crumpled white collarless shirt showing beneath his homespun jacket. The Pulo rebel produced an unlabeled bottle and two tin cups from the basket and glanced toward Cord. 'It is *zu* — rice wine. You will join me?'

Cord nodded, and his host poured a generous measure of white spirit into each cup, then handed him one. Nam Ree raised his cup in a perfunctory toast and they drank, the potent *zu* burning its way down Cord's throat, its taste a mixture of high-proof cider and distilled aniseed. Nam Ree smacked his lips, poured another measure into each cup, and then his button-nosed face crinkled into an encouraging smile. 'You have gone to a great deal of trouble to meet me, Mr. Cord. Why?'

'The obvious reason,' said Cord, his dignity partly undermined by the need to move into a more comfortable position. 'To hear why you want to sabotage the Thamaung project, and to find how we can change the situation.'

'To find my price?' Nam Ree sipped

lightly at his cup, the pale lamplight accentuating his high cheekbones and deep-set eyes. 'Have I said I'm against the project?'

'You've grabbed every chance of stirring up trouble that's come your way in the last couple of weeks,' said Cord bluntly.

Nam Ree shrugged. 'Perhaps it would be better to say I am concerned with the welfare of the people of this *ching*. I am one of them, you knew that?'

'I knew it. Does it come under 'concern with welfare' to fake a radio call and bring in the army?' Cord made no attempt to hide his feelings. 'The man who did that wasn't thinking of 'welfare,' Nam Ree. He was deliberately provoking the villagers. The rest is worse. One man is shot and wounded to keep the trouble boiling. And now another is murdered, for no clear reason.'

'You disappoint me.' Nam Ree frowned and set his cup aside. 'This much I will say, Mr. Cord. I was not responsible for the wounding of Myi Teri, even though the result was useful. Who fired that shot is a mystery I would like to solve.

And — yes — I have heard of the killing of the radioman, Donaldson. But again I had no hand in it. Such a solution might be useful to you, but,' he shook his head, appeared ready to add more, then changed his mind.

'But you faked the radio call,' Cord persisted. 'The villagers were ready to return to work, so you did the one thing calculated to wreck the situation.'

Nam Ree drew his knees up toward his chin and sat pondering for a moment. 'Mr. Cord, I will be frank with you, for the simple reason that we are alone and later I will deny every word I say. I sent the message to Captain Paya at Nanshu. Certain — friends of mine organized the strike which stopped work at the resettlement area.'

'Hell, man, for what reason?'

'I do not want the Pulo people to leave the valley.' The rebel leader glanced around him, casually changing the subject. 'I called this the Cave of Bats. That was not strictly accurate. It is one small part of a long network of many caves. We find them useful.'

'For free board and lodging?' Cord studied the man, more impressed than he cared to admit by the calm, unhurried assurance he exhibited. 'Is this what bothers you? Knowing that when the valley floods, you'll be flushed from your burrow?'

Nam Ree laughed aloud, the sound echoing down into the distance of the cave. 'Believe me, all this would be much easier if you'd accept the fact that I work only for the interests of my people.' He grew suddenly more serious. 'I have grown used to anything displeasing to the authorities in this area being automatically labeled my doing. But you of all people should understand. Do you not remember the preamble to the charter of your United Nations? The magnificent determination to 'reaffirm faith in fundamental human rights'? Or that vision of 'better standards of life in larger freedom'?'

'It goes on,' said Cord, talking with the mild weariness of a man who'd played this particular badger game many times before. 'It talks of the need to practice tolerance and live together in peace with one another as good neighbors.'

'One does not always equal the other.' Nam Ree made it a statement without malice or emotion. 'Let me tell you a little about myself to illustrate. I became a soldier because there was a war. Afterward I was able to go back to the university where — yes — where I did well. I was a lecturer in political economy, Mr. Cord. But I returned here, to be a school teacher again — perhaps a foolish decision, but my own. For two years I taught school and then . . . ' He shrugged. 'Let us say I tried for my own vision of that larger freedom, tried too soon, too much like an amateur, which is why I sit here in this — this burrow.'

'I'm more interested in the reason why nine men who came here to help shape these 'better standards' are being held for barter.'

'The ultimatum about the dam.' Nam Ree made a polite murmuring noise. '*Ma kaung* — that was made by Myi Teri when a bullet had just been taken from his leg. Some would say he had reason.

All that was originally planned was that your people should be held as a guarantee against blood being shed — our blood.'

'But now things have gotten out of control, haven't they?' said Cord evenly. 'Bad planning again — or something else neither of us understands?'

The rebel gave a wry grin. 'Do you expect an answer to that?'

'Probably not. But there's a way out of it all. If Myi Teri frees the men at the tunnel, then that part will be finished, forgotten. I guarantee it. If he doesn't . . . '

'Threats, Mr. Cord?'

'Facts. The U.N. doesn't like its civilian personnel being endangered. Supposing the General Assembly pressed for action — well — the Burmese army could call on any help it needed from outside members.'

'They might not be the only ones who could receive help,' growled Nam Ree. Then he stopped and eyed Cord speculatively. 'I have nothing against your dam or your tunnel, Mr. Cord. But I need time, time for reasons of my own.' He held up one hand to forestall interruption. 'If work was to halt on the tunnel for a season and then resume, I could guarantee you would have all the workers you needed and an end to the expense of resettlement. My people could still fashion a good life here, even if it was not a valley life.'

'If work were to halt' — Cord made it plain he was barely toying with the idea — 'if it did, how long would you want?'

'Three months.'

It came too smoothly, too quickly. So much reasonableness had to have a partial basis in truth. But the rest — Cord had an idea forming in his mind, a gradual, groping awareness of a whole series of unrelated fragments of information.

'The hostages at the tunnel would have to be released. Once that was done, the rest could be considered.'

'*Ma hok-pu* — no! It is not enough.' Nam Ree shook his head, but he was now openly bargaining. 'There would have to be a public announcement that work was to — to temporarily halt. The soldiers would have to go.'

'No.' Cord was iron firm. 'You'd have to take our word that if the hostages were released and Myi Teri's men left the tunnel area, we would be prepared to talk, and that no outside labor would be brought in to attempt to complete the tunnel.'

'And the soldiers?'

'They would stay to protect the project team. But there would be no increase in their numbers, and no man would be arrested for what has happened.'

Nam Ree rose and clapped him vigorously on the shoulder. 'On that I will agree. I can get word to Myi Teri tonight, and you can tell your people that the hostages will be released tomorrow morning.' He paused, his eyes glinting strangely for a man who, on the face of things, might appear to have given up much and gained only a little. 'I will add a warning, Mr. Cord. I am said to have fifty men at my command. The figure is an exaggeration one way and an understatement in another. The Pulos are my strength — all of them. If our bargain is broken, you will know what I mean.'

He picked up the lamp, a signal that the meeting was over. Cord rose stiffly from the ground, faced him, and said, 'You'll find out I'm right.'

'I will be there to see for myself.' Nam Ree turned down the wick of the lamp. 'I will take you back to your vehicle, then you will be guided part of the way back. I would not try to find this place again. It would be difficult, almost impossible, definitely unwise.'

Cord followed Nam Ree to the cave entrance. Going back down the hillside was made easier with the lamp's pale beam, and he stumbled only once on the way. The three men who'd brought him to the rendezvous were still lounging beside the jeep.

Nam Ree gave them a brief nod, then turned back to Cord. 'One last piece of advice before you go — and, remember, I have been a reasonable man tonight, though you accused me of shooting my own people to gain capital. You are interested in a certain young woman.'

His voice became cold, dispassionate, all but empty of inflection. 'For your own sake I would advise you against such attentions; the result could be harmful.'

'Harmful?' The surprise warning left Cord bewildered.

By the time he'd recovered, it was too late. Nam Ree was heading back into the darkness accompanied by one of the Pulos. The other two had moved around in front of Cord, barring the way. He shrugged, climbed into the jeep, waited until the men had joined him, then started the engine.

The trip was almost a carbon copy of the previous one — no lights, finger-pointing directions. Only the route was different. Cord strove to think as he drove, to shape and mold the half-formed understanding that had gradually come to him.

Three months, Nam Ree had said. Three months — long enough for the unalterable cycle of nature. He remembered the map he'd seen in Lewis' office on the day he'd arrived — which was only yesterday, though it seemed an age longer.

Just one winding hill road led into the Thamaung Valley and the vast range of hills and pocket-sized hollows which surrounded it. Take away the road, and the only reasonable approach from the rest of Burma was from the west, across the flat country of the Sihrong to the Dolpha Ridge. But Lake Mawtayn was over there, flooding over when each cycle of snow melted in the high Himalayas to rush in swollen, ice-cold torrents toward its basin. And when Lake Mawtayn flooded over, it made the vast area of marsh and bush of the Sihrong an impassable swamp.

With the Thamaung tunnel completed, Lake Mawtayn would be tamed. Without the tunnel, less than three weeks would see the entire district isolated from the rest of the country, isolated except for one easily blocked, easily held road. There might be paths through the mountains to the north and south, but a few determined men would be enough to seal these. To the east? Cord pursed his lips at the thought of the massive, eager intervention which might come from the direction of the Chinese border.

What did Nam Ree want? A short-lived glory of power before the Sihrong dried again and he was overwhelmed? It was possible; it was the type of heroic self-engineered martyrdom which could appeal to some men. Or he might want only what he claimed, for his people to retain their heritage in the valley despite its alteration.

There was a third choice, the Chinese. But would they be interested enough? The valley had beauty and grandeur, but little else beyond its people and their meager crops. Unless the thing went deeper, far deeper . . .

He was still puzzling, wrestling with a shapeless fog of probability, when the Pulo by his side gave a grunt and signaled him to stop. He pulled up, the two men got out, and one of them pointed to the right.

'That way, the river. Not far.' The Pulo's teeth flashed in a brief farewell and the two men left him, vanishing into the night. He switched on the jeep's headlights and sat for a moment, trying to establish his bearings. He was at the edge of a well-defined track, with the marks of wheel ruts plain to be seen.

He sighed, gave up, and began driving. If he could have had five minutes with Andrew Beck, five minutes to let that fat, untidy genius pick his mind, his memory, and his doubts, the whole thing would quickly become a charted reality. But Beck was half a world away.

* * *

The rifleman opened up half a mile further on, where the track skirted the edge of a twenty-foot drop into the bed of a small, almost dry *chaung* stream. The familiar staccato spang of bullets hitting metal, close metal, jerked Cord back to instant reality. The second shot smashed through the windshield, showering him with splintered glass, and the third hit the nearside front tire. The next moment the steering wheel jerked and shuddered in his hands, the jeep spun around out of control, and then the whole world tilted as the vehicle went over and down.

Cord clung to the wheel in sheer automatic reflex action. Then, as the jeep began to roll, his numbed senses reacted to the new threat of being crushed and smashed beneath the jeep's weight, of being impaled on that steering column. He let go of the wheel, catapulting himself clear with every atom of strength in his wiry frame. But even as he acted, he knew it was too late.

The jeep landed upside down at the bottom of the *chaung* in a crash of torn, smashed-in metal, Cord partly beneath it and lying on his back, pinned into the soft mud of the trickling stream, knowing he should be dead, filled with wonder at the fact he was alive. The noise died away in a last rattle of dislodged earth and stones; the engine had stopped; and the only sound to disturb the new silence was the slow, steady tick of the electric fuel pump.

The pump — a fresh horror swept over him as he thought of the fuel being forced into the carburetor, of it dripping out onto hot metal, the vaporizing, the first flash of flame, the exploding tank which would follow. He jerked in a savage attempt to free himself, then sank back again with a sob as he realized his position. He was lying with the twisted metal of the jeep's body pressing diagonally across his ribs, his head and shoulders clear, his body from the waist down trapped within. Cord tried again, tried until every muscle in his body seemed about to rupture, until the veins in his neck bulged and pulsated.

It was useless — and the pump still ticked its remorseless threat of incineration. He sniffed, caught the first faint tang of vapor, fought back a feeling of panic, and tried his only remaining hope. His legs, at least, were free to move within the jeep's confines. He brought them together, used his right shoe to lever off the left shoe, repeated the process, then flexed his toes within his thin nylon socks.

The right foot gave him the better reach. He brought it up until he felt the instrument panel, twisted his body to gain a better working angle — and was rewarded by a slash of vivid agony running through his chest. He fought against the pain and kept on working with that right foot, twisting his leg around the steering column, concentrating every particle of sensitivity he possessed into those searching toes. They found a hard, blunt knob. The light switch — it had to be the light switch and it gave him his bearings. His toes edged gently on until they contacted another protruding shape. He felt first one side, then the other, and gave a short grunt of relief. He had the ignition key.

The trickiest part of all was feeling and working with his foot until the key was jammed between his first and second toes. Then he slowly turned his foot through a forty-five-degree angle, heard the switch click, and the tick of the pump stop as the electrical circuit was broken.

Cord lay back. A last vague wondering thought of the rifle-man coming down and finishing him began entering his mind as he passed out.

* * *

The pain in his chest was still there when he came around. But it was down to a dull ache. He was lying propped against a rock with something warm wrapped around him and a fiery trickle of spirits was going down his throat. He coughed, spluttered with fresh pain, shook his head to clear his brain, and heard a whistling sigh of relief.

'Welcome back . . . ' Maurice North's face, a pale blur against the night sky, was the first thing Cord saw as he opened his eyes. The mine manager took a cigarette from his mouth and placed it between Cord's lips. 'Here — fair exchange.' As Cord took a first shallow draw, North picked up a brandy flask from the ground, took a swallowing gulp, and wiped his mouth on his sleeve.

Cord gradually became more aware of his surroundings. He was out of the *chaung*. The 'rock' he was propped against was one of the rear wheels of the Ronul mine truck and he'd been wrapped in an old, oil-smelling rug. The two Pulos who had guided him down from the ridge stood a little way off, silhouetted by the truck's lights, talking quietly to North's Burmese driver.

North followed his glance and nodded. 'Thank them, not me. I came along the track about ten minutes ago and they waved me down. We hauled the jeep off you with a rope from the truck. How do you feel?'

'Lousy.' Cord forced a shaky grin, then made some gentle, exploratory movements. His arms and legs were intact. Only the ache in his chest remained — that, and a throbbing, pounding headache. 'Where are we anyway?'

'A couple of miles from the ford crossing, about ten miles from the Thamaung camp.' North squatted by him patiently, refusing to hurry or be hurried. 'I'm no doctor, but I'd say you've broken a couple of ribs. Even at that, you're lucky.' He gestured toward the Pulos. 'According to them, they heard shots and came along to find out what was going on. Otherwise . . . '

Otherwise he might have lain there until he died — or until the sniper had put in an appearance, which could have amounted to the same thing. Cord hoisted himself into more of a sitting position and accepted another swallow of brandy.

'Somebody cut loose at me with a rifle from the hill. The Pulos didn't see anyone taking off?'

'No — if he heard them coming, he'd probably duck out quietly.' The mine manager shook his head. 'Well, at least you can't blame Nam Ree for this affair.'

Cord accepted it, with reservations. 'How did you happen along?'

'I'm on my way to the project camp.' North gave an angry frown. 'I want to find out what the hell Prinetti's been up to. I was away from the mine for a spell this evening. When I got back, I found Prinetti had paid us a visit. Seems he practically knocked the daylights out of Tan Das, my foreman, then drove away again.'

Cord felt a ripple of grim amusement.

The bearded Italian had been spoiling for trouble, but he hadn't expected him to take quite such drastic action. 'And Tan Das?'

'Don't ask me where he is. He'd packed up and gone by the time I arrived,' growled North. 'Anyway, the best thing I can do now is load you aboard the truck and head into Frajon. Feel up to it?'

Cord managed to get to his feet with a minimum of assistance, and attempted to thank the two Pulos. They shrugged and watched impassively while North and the mine driver helped him into the cab, and were still standing by the side of the track as the truck drove off.

'Well?' North glanced at him curiously as they traveled along. 'Did you get what you wanted there?' He saw Cord's eyes flicker toward their driver and set him at ease on that score. 'Tu Baw's been at the mine longer than I have — and he carried your message to Nam Ree.'

The name, at least, registered with the man. He flashed them a quick grin, then resumed his attention on the track.

'Lewis' men are being released tomorrow,' said Cord. He hesitated, then decided to go on. 'We've fixed up — well — what you could call a temporary truce. I'll keep back the details until we get to the camp, no sense in dredging through it twice. But I can tell you why Prinetti came out to see Tan Das.' He did, starting with the story of the rifle, going on through his version of the rock fall in the mine gallery, remorselessly ignoring North's initial and outraged disbelief, accepting the silence with which the end of his account was received.

North lit a cigarette and puffed on it angrily for almost a minute — and a minute can be a long time. Then, still staring out at their headlight beams biting into the night, he gave an impulsive sigh. 'But why — can you tell me? The mine's played out. You know that as well as I do. And the rest — even if you're right and Tan shot Myi Teri, what did he gain by it?'

'He whipped up an extra bowl of trouble,' said Cord shortly. 'Does he know Nam Ree?'

'Yes, but outside of Captain Paya and the army, most people do.'

'Maybe Nam Ree wasn't going far enough for Tan Das's liking. The one thing I can't lay against Tan Das is Donaldson's murder; he was busy trying to bring your mine down on top of me when that happened. Come to that, he was probably behind the rifle which nearly finished me tonight. Look, North, you know the man. Ever thought he might have friends over to the east?'

'In Red China?' North considered this seriously. 'No, he never gave any hint of it, didn't seem interested in anything but his job. You think that's the angle? That he's one of the boys they slip over the border to raise general hell?'

'For want of a better one.' Cord was instinctively against parading the possibilities. 'How friendly is he with Nam Ree?'

'He isn't as far as I know.' North questioned their driver for a moment in low, fluent Burmese, then shook his head. 'They met a couple of times at the mine, nothing more. Cord, you're forgetting something. Nam Ree has a contact at the project camp. No use asking me who he is, because I don't know. But couldn't he be your real troublemaker?'

'He or she . . . '

'She?'

Cord shrugged. Nam Ree's parting warning was still strong in his mind. 'Let's say I believe in casting a wide net.'

North stared in dismay at Cord's hard yet still youthful face. 'Do you trust anyone, Cord? Really trust them?'

He didn't get an answer. Somehow he didn't seem to expect one.

* * *

It was almost an hour after midnight when they arrived at the project camp. North handled the preliminaries, rousing Dr. Holst and Paya before he went off on his own business. The Doctor arrived cursing and sleepy-eyed, jacket and trousers pulled over his pajamas; but Paya, who reached the surgery minutes later, was his usual immaculately dressed self.

A prodding, grumbling examination by the Thamaung Doctor showed that Cord had been luckier than they'd anticipated. His rib cage was badly bruised, one rib had a possible hairline crack, but that was all. Holst injected a pain-killing shot of morphine, then scratched his head.

'If I leave it as it is, which is best, you should not be moving around too much. Otherwise, I should strap this up.'

'I want to stay mobile,' Cord told him.

Holst sighed, produced a wide roll of bandage, and set to work while his patient talked.

'So they will let Lewis and the others go free in the morning — good!' Captain Paya was relieved but cautious. 'And your side of the bargain?'

'No action against the villagers, no imported labor, no additional military, and we start immediate talks with them to iron out the situation.'

'*To-pan* — you sound like a trade-union official.' Paya watched with detached interest while another layer of bandage was tightened around Cord's rib cage. 'Hmm. Was it an easy path, the route you took to meet Nam Ree?'

'It scared years off my life.' Cord winced as Dr. Holst jerked the strapping. 'Even if I wanted to, I couldn't guide you back the same way. I didn't know where I was half the time.'

Paya tried to cloak his disappointment. 'And this man, Tan Das — as you say, he could be at the root of several things.'

'Too many,' agreed Cord. 'It's what he may try to do next that worries me.'

'This could be a very delicate time.' Paya chewed his lower lip, immediately concerned. 'If you have some pointer . . . '

'I haven't. I can't even suggest anything.'

'Then I will suggest instead,' growled Dr. Holst, finishing his task and leaning back. 'If, as a patient, you are such a fool as to refuse my advice and either die from pneumonia, pleurisy, or a pierced lung that is your affair. But if there could be more trouble ahead, then any unessential personnel like Mrs. Prinetti and her child should be gotten out of here. The first could leave when the helicopter makes its return flight.'

Cord blinked. 'What helicopter?'

'The one which is to bring in a government forensic expert. He is being flown up from Rangoon,' said Paya with a note of relief in his voice. 'I was advised of this only tonight. There will also be a United Nations official, an authority on ethnic and cultural problems, whatever use that is supposed to be. Still, it means we are now to be not quite alone, and it is a change of heart I welcome.' He dragged one of the now familiar radio message slips from his pocket. 'This also came, for you. It is a good code, Mr. Cord. I have already tried hard to break it.'

As a code it was, in fact, simple enough, provided you knew the basic transposition key. Otherwise, anything short of an electronic computer-analyzer would have rejected it as gibberish. Cord read it through, slowly translating it to himself a word at a time, no easy mental task. When he'd finished, he folded the message slip and pushed it into a pocket, his face immobile.

Andrew Beck was worried, which in itself meant trouble. A routine meeting of the U.N. Economic and Social Council was scheduled in one week's time, and word had wafted to the Field Reconnaisance team that a delegate renowned for his bull-at-a-gate awkwardness was going to throw a surprise question about Thamaung into the debate. The helicopter flight was Beck's idea, and the 'ethnic and cultural authority' aboard it was Karl Steeven, Cord's regular running mate when the going became heavy or speed was paramount.

'Important news?' murmured Paya hopefully.

Cord shook his head. 'Just someone telling me to get a move on. Where's Maurice North?'

'He went to see Prinetti.' Dr. Holst tidied away the last of his equipment and helped Cord back into his shirt. He looked up as the door opened, and his face brightened. 'Come in, Marian. Provided you aren't another patient, you're welcome.'

Marian Frey entered the room and closed the door behind her. She had dressed in her workaday shirt and slacks, but her hair was only combed back roughly and her face was bare of makeup. She crossed toward Cord, concern in her eyes. 'I've heard what happened,' she told him. 'I wasn't sleeping, and when people started rushing around I got curious. You — you're all right?'

'Bent but more or less unbroken.' Cord gave her a quick, reassuring grin. 'I was just going to find North.'

'Maurice? That won't be hard. He's having some sort of a row with Victor Prinetti. I heard them at it when I passed that way.' She eyed the bandages with concern as he finished fastening the shirt. 'Doctor, should he be moving around?'

'Why ask me?' grumbled Holst. 'When a man has the mentality of a mule he should call for a veterinarian, not a doctor.' He picked up Cord's jacket from the table and threw it toward him. 'I ask you all to do me a favor and cause no more trouble until after breakfast. The human body is like a battery — it needs regular rest and recharging. My battery is low and I wish to sleep without calls from people who — who want me to act as a damned mechanic who does running repairs.'

Captain Paya nodded weary and wholehearted agreement, and they went out, leaving the medical man still swearing to himself. Paya lingered with them only a moment in the chill air of the compound, then excused himself. He had that message to send off to Myitkyina, and for once he was happy at the thought of what he could report.

Cord and the girl went on alone, heading for Prinetti's house.

'Lona still asleep?' asked Cord conversationally.

Marian smiled and nodded. 'It takes a lot to disturb her. Talos, is it true — about the Pulos, I mean? That they're releasing the hostages?'

'Tomorrow, according to Nam Ree.' He glanced at his watch. It was two A.M. 'Today now.' He turned too quickly toward her as he spoke and winced at the result.

She took his arm in a quick gesture of sympathy and support, and he looked at her for a moment, remembering Nam Ree's warning, almost reluctant to probe its meaning. Which girl had the Pulo rebel tried to protect, and why? Marian, who held a special place as Maurice North's friend, or Lona Marsh, who seemed so patently cleared of suspicion?

'Got another problem?' asked the girl by his side.

'Just wondering about Nam Ree,' he said slowly. 'Ever met him?'

'Once, out at Ronul when I arrived unexpectedly.' She gave him an oddly quizzical look. 'Maurice asked me not to talk about it. Why?'

'Curiosity.' He gave her a lopsided grin. 'He must have made a pretty tough school teacher.'

* * *

There was no doubt about Prinetti's household being awake. Lights burned at the windows and they heard the rumble of raised voices against the background of a crying child even before they reached the door. Anna Prinetti answered Cord's knock, a dressing gown pulled over her nightclothes, a look of relief on her face when she saw them.

'Come in,' she urged. 'They are in the kitchen. I can get no sense out of them, and now they have awakened my son. Men!' She rolled her eyes in despair.

They went in while the woman hurried off toward the child's room, soothing, motherly noises already coming from her lips. The row in the kitchen died away as they entered. Maurice North stood near the cabinet, an angry flush on his face. Prinetti, a picturesque apparition in a multi-colored dressing gown, his bearded face still topped by the turban-like bandage, his feet bare, stood at the opposite end of the room, his mouth twisted in an attempt at a welcoming smile.

'Well?' Cord glanced from one man to the other. 'Got it settled yet?'

'Settled!' North gave a growl. 'So far it's taken me all this time to get a word in now and again.'

'Prinetti?'

The Italian made a wide, all-embracing gesture with his hands. 'He comes into my house in the middle of the night like — like an angry bear, and asks me why I beat up his foreman. *Al contrario!* All I did was hit Tan Das a couple of times, like I hit any man who tries to bend an iron bar over my skull, especially now, when it hurts already.' He cleared his throat, remembered the girl, and spat politely into the kitchen sink. '*Pazienza!* I ask Signor North in return why he doesn't know what is going on under his own nose.'

The bearded foreman crossed to a cupboard, opened it, reached in, and tossed an attaché-case-sized bundle toward them. Wrapped in waterproof sheeting, it hit the top of the kitchen table with a solid thud. 'This was hidden in the man's hut, Signor Cord. I was keeping it to show you first.'

Cord unwrapped the bundle and unsnapped the lid of the heavy, oblong case inside. Then he gave a soft whistle. There was no more need to wonder about the source of the low-power pirate signals from the valley. It was a neat, compact, battery-powered transmitter-receiver — and losing it would be a major blow to Tan Das.

There was a second, smaller package beside it. An oilskin pouch contained a money clip crammed with high-denomination kyat notes and a mint condition 7.62 Nagant revolver. Cord flipped the weapon open — all the chambers were loaded.

North took the money clip, rippled the kyat notes between finger and thumb, and gave a shake of his head. 'There's more here than I earn in a couple of years.'

'Expenses,' said Cord briefly.

The mine manager bit his lip, nodded, then walked slowly toward Prinetti. 'He — well — I'm sorry,' he said awkwardly. 'I only knew him as a good workman.'

'He was one damn good workman,' agreed Prinetti solemnly. Then he held up his hand for silence, listened, and beamed. 'Young Victor is quiet again. Maybe if I ask Anna, she can find a bottle of *vino* for us. Okay?' He chuckled as they agreed. 'Signor North, I will tell you this before we are through — once I found that radio and the gun, I wished I'd hit Tan Das one damn sight harder.'

* * *

The morning mist had thinned from the valley's mouth before the first signs of activity began on the tunnel side of the dam. At last, a small procession of figures began wending their way down toward the parapet walk and minutes later the first of the Thamaung hostages crossed over. The hostage glanced around the group waiting to meet them, saw Lona Marsh, and caught her up in an enthusiastic hug.

The others followed, their mood a mixture of relief and delight. Henry Lewis was the last to arrive, striding over with an ornately carved walking stick in one hand.

'A present from Myi Teri,' he said self-consciously, once the handshakes were over. 'He says they'll begin leaving the tunnel camp in about fifteen minutes.'

'Everything's ready for them.' Cord thumbed over his shoulder toward the Pulo village. No one had heard the actual return, but the women of Frajon were back, smoke curled again from the thatched huts, even the children swarmed in play around the tiny vegetable plots.

'How did you do it?' asked Lewis emotionally, looking from Cord to Paya, then back again. 'They simply woke us at dawn this morning and said we were being set free, that there would be no more trouble.'

'Mr. Cord has the answer,' said Paya with a sudden flash of his white, even teeth. 'It is good to see this part, at least, ended. Now there is a meal waiting at the compound, and once the villagers have come down from the tunnel I will post a fresh guard around it.'

'Won't that . . . '

'Cause trouble?' Cord stopped him with a shake of his head. 'We're not finished yet, Lewis, but we've got this stage more or less sorted out.'

'Apart from a murder,' murmured Paya reproachfully.

'What do you mean?' Lewis' mouth dropped open in surprise.

'Your radioman, Donaldson,' said the soldier briefly. 'He was killed yesterday, in his bedroom; but I suggest the details can keep for the moment.'

The joy had vanished from the project chief's face. 'Donaldson! But why?'

'I'm hoping you might know,' said Cord. 'Didn't he originally have a meeting scheduled with you for yesterday?'

'That?' Lewis began walking with them, moving with the slow, dragging pace of a man who suddenly felt old beyond his years. 'It hardly matters. I was going to lecture him about irresponsible behavior.' He shrugged and gave a deep sigh. 'You remember the fuss the Pulos made because some of our people visited their holy *ku* up in the valley? Donaldson was the leading light in the expedition.'

'Hardly a motive for murder,' mused Paya. 'Still, if I were a superstitious man or one of the old guard among the Pulos, I might say the nats had done this to express their anger.'

'Nats?' Cord glanced at him with a mixture of exasperation and bewilderment.

'The nature spirits,' Lewis explained dully. 'Many of the Pulos are still animists — I told you that before, Cord.'

'Did you ask Donaldson why he'd gone there?'

'No. I simply told him I'd heard and that he was to see me.' A flush touched Lewis' cheeks at Cord's persistence. 'He was to submit a report in writing when he came. Does it matter? He may have been the leader, but there were two others with him.'

'Then we'd better see them,' said Cord, knowing a rising excitement. 'Donaldson managed to mumble a couple of words to Marian before he died. She thought he said 'notes,' and it seemed to fit because he'd been writing. But supposing he was trying to say 'nats'?'

Lewis obviously thought he was mad. Paya had begun applying himself with a gloomy dedication to the task of examining his fingernails.

Cord didn't care. Andy Donaldson had

been to the Pulo shrine and now he was dead. Was it because the young Scot had stumbled on something up there, something too important for him to be allowed to live to talk about it?

A new wave of almost savage confidence swept through him. He'd begun to realize a mistake he'd made, but he was also beginning to realize why.

6

Myi Teri was a man of his word. The initial trickle of villagers began crossing the river at the time he'd promised, disdaining the parapet route, splashing across the shallow river ford a little way below the shattered remnants of the plank walkway. The headman was one of the first, being carried on a rough litter, his bandaged leg covered by a blanket; and as the Pulos began arriving, the six rifles looted from the police post were quietly handed over to some of the watching soldiers.

'We've got those, and a few shotguns they looted from the compound area,' grumbled Captain Paya, pacing restlessly up and down Lewis' office a little later. 'Perhaps I should be satisfied — all this, and Prinetti seizing that radio. But these Pulos still have their own firearms hidden somewhere.' He shrugged. 'Most will be rust-eaten antiques, but they are still lethal. If I could question just a few of these villagers . . . '

'I'd bet you wouldn't get anything out of them. What matters is they're back.' Talos Cord eased deeper into his chair and glanced toward Henry Lewis.

Freshly shaven and in clean clothes, a good meal under his belt, the U.N. project chief was back behind his desk.

'All arranged for the tunnel inspection?' Cord asked.

Lewis nodded. His face was still tired and lined, but a trace of his old, driving spirit was once again apparent. He pencil ticked the written list before him. 'Prinetti should be up there now. But we'd have seen it if they'd been making any move to plant explosives.'

'Call the inspection a form of insurance,' murmured Cord lazily. 'They had a little time to themselves, remember.'

Captain Paya grunted agreement. 'And once you're satisfied, I'll have a guard on.'

There was a soft tap at the door and it opened. Lona Marsh looked in. 'They're both here now, Mr. Lewis.'

'Good.' Lewis gave a nod of satisfaction. 'Show them in.'

The two project men who entered seemed faintly puzzled at their summons. Lewis waved them toward chairs placed in readiness in front of his desk and made a brief introduction. 'John Holly and Peter Brun, the men who went with Donaldson to the Pulo shrine.'

Cord nodded. Both had been listed in Marian Frey's notes. Holly, a dark, plump New Zealander, was a rock driller. Peter Brun, a stocky, fair-haired Austrian, was an electrical engineer. He placed both men in their early thirties.

'You've heard what happened to Andy?' he asked abruptly. The men exchanged glances and then nodded. 'I asked Mr. Lewis to get you over here because we need your help.'

'Us?' Holly gave a grimace of surprise. 'Look, mister, we were both in the ruddy tunnel . . . '

'When he was killed,' Cord agreed. 'What I'm interested in is your trip to the Pulo shrine.

'The *hu?*' The New Zealander was

incredulous. 'Hell, that couldn't have anything to do with it.'

'Better let us worry about that,' said Cord perfunctorily. He pointed toward the other man. 'How about you, Brun? Like to tell me what happened?'

The Austrian stroked his chin. 'There is not much to tell. Andy suggested the trip and we agreed. I wanted to take some photographs of the place and Johnny,' he glanced half-humorously at his companion, 'well, he had nothing better to do.'

'You've got the photographs?' queried Lewis.

Brun shook his head. 'I have still to send them out to Myitkyina to be processed. But they were just general views around the cave.'

'Were all three of you always together?' asked Cord, his hopes beginning to fade. 'Did you see anything out of the ordinary, anything which struck you as odd?'

'Nope.' Holly was heavily positive. 'And we stayed together. Man, as a trip it was a washout. Then after we got back,' he shrugged, 'well, nobody had told us the *ku* was off limits.'

'It wasn't,' said Lewis sharply. 'I simply expected adult common sense at an awkward time.'

'I'm sorry.' Holly sounded more bored than penitent. 'We didn't mean any harm.'

Peter Brun leaned forward suddenly, his face thoughtful. 'Mr. Cord, there is this — one little time when Andy was not beside us. Just as we were about to leave, he told us he'd left his pocket-flashlight behind in the cave. He went back for it.'

Holly came out of his lethargy and snapped his fingers. 'Hey, that's right. I'd forgotten. We waited for him at the truck and he was back in about a minute. He more or less went straight in and straight out again. Look, why all the questions anyway? According to him, the report he was going to give the old man . . . ' He stopped, winced a little under the project chief's icy glare, and corrected himself. 'I mean to Mr. Lewis here would get us off the hook.'

'Off the hook?' Paya was puzzled.

'Clear us, wipe the slate . . . '

'Did he say why?' probed Cord with a new intensity.

Brun answered. 'No, but surely the report he was ordered to make . . . '

'There's no report,' said Lewis shortly. 'Mr. Cord believes it was taken by the same person who murdered Donaldson.'

'Well, isn't there a copy?' demanded Holly. 'Can't you ask Lona what it was about?'

He saw the surprise he'd caused and for once had to flounder for words. 'What I mean is — well — he said he'd get Lona to type it for him.'

Cord was already on his way to the door. 'Lona, would you come in?'

She came in carrying her shorthand notebook and pencil and glanced inquiringly toward Lewis.

'Lona, Mr. Holly has suggested that Andy Donaldson may have asked you to — ah — to type a report of his visit to the Pulo shrine.' Lewis ran his tongue over his lips, patently embarrassed. 'Do you know anything about this?'

'No, I'm sorry.' Her face showed a

brief secretarial concern. 'But I'd have done it if he'd asked.'

'He made no mention at all of it to you?'

The girl frowned. 'Well — he did say there might be a fairly longish memo he'd want me to type. But that was a few days ago. He never appeared with it.' She paused, her hands still hugging the book and pencil. 'Is there anything else, Mr. Lewis? I thought I'd go over to the mess hall for coffee. I told Marian I would meet her.'

'Yes, that's all — and thank you.' Lewis waited until the door closed, then gave a faint shrug. 'No luck there, I'm afraid.'

'Maybe he didn't get around to doing it after all,' admitted Holly. Then he snapped his fingers again. 'Hey, he could have asked Anna Prinetti. She does a spot of typing now and again for Dr. Holst.'

'You're sure?' asked Cord.

'I've seen her do it.'

Cord lit a cigarette, drew on it, then rose from his chair. 'Well, we'll check. Thanks for coming over.'

'That's okay.' Holly nudged his companion and they got up to go.

Cord went with them to the door, and as they departed, he made a quick check that the outer office was empty. When he returned, he closed the door behind him again.

'Another blank, unless Mrs. Prinetti can help.' Lewis was despondent. 'Well, shall we go and see her?'

'Maybe we should wait until her husband gets back,' suggested Paya cautiously. 'Prinetti can be temperamental.'

Cord had walked over to the window. He stared out of it for a moment, then swung back toward them. 'Paya, you told me you could vouch for Lona Marsh for almost an hour before Donaldson was killed . . . '

'Until I was told he had been found dying,' agreed the soldier. 'And you can hardly think of Mrs. Prinetti as a suspect . . . '

'I'm thinking of her as a typist,' said Cord stonily. 'You said Lona was working throughout that hour. Where was she working — and where were you?'

'She was in her office, just outside this door,' said the soldier impatiently. 'I was in one of the offices a little way along the corridor, the electrical section room. It was handy.'

'So you didn't see her!'

'But I heard her,' retorted Paya. 'The typewriter . . . '

'You heard a typewriter,' Cord emphasized. 'Did you see who was using it? Did you see Lona in her office before you went to Donaldson's room?'

Captain Paya swallowed and shook his head. 'No, but . . . '

'You gave her work to do, and then after the killing she turned up at the staff block,' said Cord heavily. 'In between times you heard a typewriter, and then afterward she handed you the finished job. That's what it amounts to, isn't it?'

'You mean it could have been Anna Prinetti who typed the material for Paya?' Henry Lewis kneaded his fingers together and tried to remain calm. 'There's only one way to find out I suppose.'

* * *

Anna Prinetti was washing clothes in the kitchen of her home when they arrived. She rubbed the last of the suds from her hands onto her apron, smiled rather nervously at them, and suggested, 'I have some coffee warming, waiting for Victor.'

Lewis shook his head. 'I'd like to ask you a couple of questions, Mrs. Prinetti. The answers could be important, very important. If you want, we could wait until your husband gets back, but . . . '

'Questions? About last night?' She bit her lip. 'Victor shouldn't have said what he did to Mr. North, but he meant well. You know that, Mr. Cord.'

'This has nothing to do with last night,' Cord reassured her. 'The questions concern you, Anna. We'll wait if you'd prefer it.'

She shook her head. 'No, there is no need. What are the questions, Mr. Lewis?'

Lewis scowled in awkward dislike of the task. 'Now we're not suggesting you've done anything wrong, Mrs. Prinetti,' he began. 'But what we — well — what we want to know is if you've ever given my secretary any help with her duties?'

'Lona?' The woman cocked her head to one side and looked more cheerful. 'A few times, yes. She is a nice girl, and I have time to spare. Was some mistake made?'

'Not by you, Anna,' said Cord cryptically. 'Did you ever do any typing for Andy Donaldson, any letter or memo about the Pulo shrine?'

She shook her head and stood toying nervously with her apron. 'I have done only one job recently. That was yesterday — work for you, Captain Paya. It was the situation report for your headquarters — two carbons and double-spacing, Lona said. I checked it through afterward and it seemed correct.'

Paya gave a whistling sigh. 'It was excellently done, Mrs. Prinetti. I had no complaints. But why did Miss Marsh ask you to type it?'

Anna Prinetti rested her still damp hands on her hips, her pleasant face flushing a little. 'She — she told me she had a headache, a migraine. She wanted to lie down for a spell.'

Cord nodded encouragingly. 'And you typed the report on her machine, in her office?' As she agreed, he went on. 'When did you see her next?'

'Outside the staff block, after poor Andy had been found.' The foreman's wife was concerned now. 'Will telling this mean trouble for Lona? She works hard, that girl . . . '

'She does,' agreed Cord dryly. 'Has she had these migraine headaches before?'

'They happen.' Mrs. Prinetti grew more and more flustered. 'Marian would know more about them, living with her. I told Lona she should ask Dr. Holst for some tablets; but she said no, that if she could lie down in a darkened room and be left alone for a little, then the headaches would go . . . '

'A nice, simple outlook,' said Cord. And convenient. He asked the woman to contact him if she remembered anything else, then they said their good-byes. As they left, she was turning back to the rest of the washing, her face still showing the same bewildered concern.

Outside the house, Paya stopped where he was and swore with a quiet, passionate concentration. 'I want another talk with this girl,' he growled. 'This time, I will be less polite than before.'

'But what happened sounds reasonable,' protested Lewis out of sheer loyalty to his secretary. He appealed to Cord. 'Don't you think this is all too much like jumping to conclusions?'

Cord stayed quiet, but Paya wasn't finished. 'I have stopped jumping to conclusions, Mr. Lewis, because every conclusion seems to leave me a bigger fool than before. But I promise you this. From now on, when I ask questions, I either get the answers I seek or the man or woman concerned goes under close arrest until this is over.'

'Well, here's somebody who seems to have no worries,' said Cord mildly, pointing to their left.

Victor Prinetti came striding toward them from the direction of the dam and beamed as he neared them.

'Everything in order?' asked Lewis anxiously.

'Jus' *excellente.*' The bearded foreman cupped finger and thumb expressively. 'I checked right through wit' that boy officer, Lieutenant — Lieutenant . . . '

'Lieutenant Maung,' said Paya a trifle coldly.

'*Grazie.* Anyway, the tunnel is not harmed and your Lieutenant has put a guard there and on the explosives magazine.'

'How was the magazine?' queried Cord.

'The lock smashed and half-a-dozen sticks of gelignite an' the same number of detonators missing.' Prinetti scratched his beard. 'Jus' what they'd need when they blew up the walk-way.' He glanced toward his home. 'You came looking for me, Signor Lewis?'

Lewis shook his head. 'No. We had a chat with your wife. Nothing important, Prinetti; she'll tell you all about it.'

The man raised an eyebrow and waited. Then, as he realized no further explanation was coming, he frowned a little. 'All right. I see you later, eh?' He walked on, looked briefly back at them after a few paces, shrugged, and went into his house.

In the same unbroken silence the three men made their way down to the mess hall. The only person in the building was Holly, the rock driller, who lounged over the remnants of a late breakfast, wild zithee plums sprinkled with chili pepper.

'Seen Lona Marsh here?' demanded Cord.

Holly gave a gentle belch and shook his head. 'I've been on my own since I arrived. Maybe she changed her mind. Haven't seen her pal either, come to that.' His interest grew. 'Want her for something, eh?' They were already on their way to the door. He shrugged, and turned back to the plums.

Outside, Paya halted, lit a cigarette, and drew on it angrily. 'Her living quarters next — and if she is not there, we know what that means.'

'You two go on,' Cord agreed. 'I'm going to try my luck among the Pulos.'

'Would she go there?' Paya was dubious.

'That's not what I've got in mind,' he told them, and turned away, leaving Lewis standing dispiritedly beside the soldier.

* * *

The Pulo village was a bustle of cheerful activity as he reached it and walked between the stilt-legged huts. He saw broad grins directed at him from the men he passed, heard the shrill, busy chatter of their womenfolk. An old and crackling radio blared music from one hut, and he could hear a child howling in another. The villagers seemed in no doubt that they'd won the clash of wills, and the matter over, they were jubilant.

A few khaki-clad soldiers wended their way through the bustle. A few hours before they'd been eying the villagers in their rifle sights. Now they were already bargaining over the price of a leaf-wrapped snack of rice or a thimble-sized cup of *zu* from the stalls set up by two business-minded hut owners.

'Talos . . . '

He heard the shout, turned, and Marian Frey waved toward him from the midst of one group. She reached him a moment later, smiling, wearing a red corduroy windbreaker jacket over a white-and-blue candy-striped shirt and a plain dark blue skirt.

'I gather they're glad to be back,' he said dryly.

'They certainly are.' She laughed. 'I came over to see if they'd need any help. But when they're not busy apologizing to me about it all, they're talking about the celebration they're going to hold.'

'Good.' The way he said it took the smile from her lips.

'What's wrong?' she asked.

'Marian, did you have any date to meet Lona this morning — for coffee at the mess hall?'

'No, why?'

'That's where she said she was going. Now we want her. Anna Prinetti was covering up for her around the time Andy was killed.'

The gray eyes widened. 'And you think . . . '

'I think she's decided it's time to get out,' said Cord bluntly. 'You'd better get back and talk to Paya.'

She nodded, turned on her heel, and went quickly away. Cord watched her for a moment, then shrugged and continued his errand.

The giant Pulo with the gold earring was on guard outside Myi Teri's hut, one hand resting lightly on the belt of his leather-sheathed *dah*. He gave a glint of recognition, but didn't move as Cord went past him, climbed the stairway to the verandah, and pushed through the rattan screen at the hut doorway.

Myi Teri lay on a couch by the smoldering fire, and he already had a visitor. Dr. Holst squatted at the foot of the couch while a young Pulo girl stood patiently in the background. She glanced toward Cord, then scurried away into the rear of the hut, vanishing behind a partition wall of woven bamboo.

Dr. Holst greeted him with a nod. 'Came along to change this leg dressing,' he said. 'It's doing fine' — a broad wink toward the headman accompanied his words — 'gives my friend here a good excuse to loaf around for a spell.'

Myi Teri lifted himself up on his elbows, his face crinkled in a polite, cautious greeting. 'There is no trouble about the truce?'

Cord shook his head. 'None. I came along for a talk.'

'Which means you can do without me.' Dr. Holst snapped his bag shut and rose. 'Remember what I said now. I don't want you trying to get up for a spell.'

The headman nodded, turned his head, and called toward the rear of the hut. The same girl, a dark-eyed well-built child in her early teens, reappeared and went to the door, holding the rattan screen open as the medical man made his exit. Then she crossed back to the couch.

'You would like tea?' asked Myi Teri.

Cord declined, but took a cheroot from a box brought by the child, and let her light it with a taper from the fire. He puffed contentedly for a moment while she did the same for Myi Teri.

'Mr. Cord, have you discovered yet who fired this shot which wounded me?' The man's face twitched. 'If it was not the soldiers . . . '

'We've an idea who it was. But we'll need more time before we're sure.'

'That is what Dr. Holst said.' Myi Teri lowered himself back on the couch, his eyes roaming around the dull interior of the hut. 'Why are you here?'

'I thought you might have a visitor. I'd like to see him.'

Myi Teri regarded him steadily for a moment, then turned laboriously on his side and spoke to the girl. She went to the hut door and looked out, then came back and shook her head. Myi Teri relaxed a little, gave a slight nod, and she disappeared into the rear of the hut. Cord heard a quiet murmur of voices, and a moment later a new figure appeared from behind the partition screen.

'Well, Mr. Cord?' Nam Ree was dressed as a villager, wearing an ankle-length *loongyi* and an old, torn jacket. He came nearer, a strangely wary expression on his face. 'I am glad my men could help you last night. I, too, would like to meet this rifleman who is plaguing us.' He shook his head. 'Still, I have kept my word. Your people have been freed and the villagers have come down from the tunnel camp. And you have kept your side of the bargain. It is a good thing when men can trust one another.'

'Can they always?' Cord puffed blandly on the cheroot. 'Your contact at the survey camp, for instance . . . '

'Presuming that I have one.' Nam Ree was still more wary than before.

'Your contact at the survey camp,' repeated Cord levelly. 'You as good as told me where to look last night, only I started off on the wrong foot. Lona Marsh is a very clever young woman, an expert at covering her tracks.'

Nam Ree regarded him quizzically, abandoning pretence. 'You think so? She will be pleased to hear it.'

From that instant Cord realized there was something definitely wrong with the situation. He'd been prepared to have the Pulo rebel deny the fact, laugh, ignore him — anything but this cheerful admission.

'Just for a spell I thought you were warning me off Marian Frey, perhaps because of North's interest in her,' he said slowly, feeling his mouth going dry, knowing that the chips must really be down when Nam Ree was so benignly confident. 'Lona was clever all right, even when it came to murder.'

If Nam Ree's response before had worried him, the man's reaction now came as a savage shock. The Pulo's mouth hardened, and he grabbed Cord by the shoulder, his free hand raised in a flat-edged threat. 'Murder? What murder, Mr. Cord? I would speak carefully. No man likes his daughter to be accused of such a thing.'

'Your daughter!' Cord was dumfounded and showed it.

'My daughter.' Nam Ree slowly lowered his hand and released his grip. But there was harsh anger in his voice. 'I think you should explain, Mr. Cord, explain quickly.'

Cord tossed the cheroot into the

fireplace embers and tried to adjust to the situation. 'I knew she was half Burmese, but . . . '

'Marsh was her mother's name. She found it convenient,' snapped the Pulo rebel. 'Now say what you mean.'

'All right. When Donaldson was murdered your — your daughter was allegedly typing in her office. She wasn't. We know that now. She had time to go to Donaldson's room and kill him.'

'For what reason?' Nam Ree's eyes still blazed like coals. 'This is all you have? This story that she was not where she should have been?'

'There's more, all pointing the same way.'

Nam Ree laughed, a deep, confident bellow which worried Cord more than the previous anger. 'I see. You are in need of a criminal to fit this crime, and you have Lona who was my ear in the project camp, a most efficient ear. She got me the radio hut key, the frequencies, the rest. But she did not kill this man.' He took a step closer, his face inches away. 'There was no reason, Mr. Cord.'

Cord saw Myi Teri watching closely in the background. The headman's face was strained and he seemed to be waiting, as if knowing what would happen next and yet uncertain whether he liked it or not. The two Pulos shared a common tension, a tension growing with every second.

'If she's innocent, then have her talk with me,' suggested Cord swiftly. 'She can help us — and you say yourself the Pulos had no hand in Donaldson's killing.'

'Help you?' Nam Ree shook his head. '*Ma hok-pu*. The time for that is over, Mr. Cord.' The hand which came out of his jacket pocket held a small, snub-nosed revolver. 'Move over to the door, but slowly,' said the Pulo rebel quietly. 'Myi Teri has had no part in what is to happen, though I am under his roof and his protection. Remember that — what you are to see is my doing.'

'You gave your word . . . '

'And I have kept it, as far as it went.' The gun still pointing steadily, Nam Ree moved with him to the door.

Cord pulled aside one corner of the

screen and looked out across the village and the dam, watching the Ridge and the tunnel's mouth with a sense of sickened anticipation.

'No one will be hurt,' said Nam Ree, talking almost to himself. 'But this is the answer, Mr. Cord. This is my way out. Just wait — and watch.' He prodded the muzzle of the gun against Cord's side, then fixed his eyes on the tunnel, breathing softly and quietly while the seconds slid past.

The tunnel mouth seemed to quiver first, like a hot-weather mirage. Then the roar reached their ears, a roar which synchronized with a spouting cloud of dust and seemed to shake the very boards beneath their feet with its violence. Over on the Ridge the dust billowed until it almost obscured the entire area of the tunnel camp. From the village around them came cries and shouts, a mixture of fear and warning, the sound of running feet, a squealing and barking of terrified dogs.

Nam Ree let out a long sigh of satisfaction. 'That is the rest of my answer, Mr. Cord. Now stay perfectly still. I could ask Myi Teri to hold you here for a little, but that would be implicating him in what has happened, and he knew as little of it as you until moments before the Doctor arrived.'

Cord felt the man move behind him, glimpsed the gun hand rise out of the corner of his eye; then the blow hit him on the back of the neck and he was knocked to his knees, dazed, his mind a red haze of pain and only vaguely aware of Nam Ree's departure. The weakness and muscular paralysis lasted only seconds, but when he pulled himself back to his feet and stood looking out of the doorway, one hand gripping the wood for support, the Pulo had vanished.

For the rest, wild confusion reigned in the village. Khaki-clad soldiers running back to their posts jostled with women rushing children toward the huts, and Pulo menfolk who stood staring toward the Ridge, their mouths open with wonderment. The dust cloud was slowly settling. The tunnel mouth had vanished, leaving in its place a scar of raw, blasted rock. A bugle sang to life over in the compound area and a whistle was blowing down near the dam.

Cord looked back into the hut. Myi Teri was still propped up on his elbows, silently watching him, his face woodenly impassive. Cord pursed his lips and went out, staggering a little as he made his way down the stairway from the verandah. Still dazed and lightheaded, he moved on through the bustle of the panic-stricken village. He was halfway toward the compound area when a command truck crammed with infantrymen skidded to a stop beside him.

'Get in.' Captain Paya reached out one long, thick arm and practically dragged him aboard. The truck shot off again, and, behind them, Cord glimpsed another, only the tip of its aerial pennant clearly visible above the huts. Paya leaned over, his face an angry mask, bellowing to make himself heard above the engine's roar. 'We're going to the tunnel. So much for your 'peaceful solution.''

He hung on as the truck bounded down the riverbank and hit the shallow ford beyond with a drenching splash of spray. 'It was Nam Ree; he was in the village.'

'You let him get away?' For a moment the soldier seemed ready to throw him out in midstream. 'I'm cordoning off the village — nobody in, nobody out.'

The truck jolted out on the Ridge side of the dam, and whined in low gear up the steep track beyond.

There were soldiers already gathered around the rubble of the tunnel entrance, Lieutenant Maung among them. He ran to meet the truck as it rolled to a halt, his face and clothes covered with a film of gray rock dust, his attitude that of a schoolboy expecting a sound thrashing.

'Well?' Paya barked the word, swinging himself down from the vehicle.

Cord followed, moving more slowly but still in time to hear the younger soldier's stumbling reply.

'The — the tunnel blew up, sir.'

'Hah! I thought it might have been mice.' Paya turned a withering glare on his subordinate. 'You checked the tunnel with Prinetti, you posted a guard — will it be too much of a strain on you to tell me how in creation this happened?'

Lieutenant Maung shook his head. 'No one passed the sentries. No one except the girl . . . '

'Lona Marsh?' Cord gripped him urgently by the arm. 'Lewis' secretary?'

'Yes.' Maung seemed close to weeping. 'But she had a permit signed by Captain Paya . . . '

'What?' Paya seemed about to burst a blood vessel. 'Maung, tell me about her. And quickly, unless you like the thought of perpetual sentry duty on this rubble heap.'

The hapless subordinate swallowed. 'The girl came up not long after Prinetti and I had finished inspecting the tunnel . . . '

'Alone?'

Maung shook his head. 'She had a man with her. He looked like one of the project men. He was certainly no Pulo.'

'Small, thin, with twisted teeth?' prompted Cord, and groaned inwardly as the young soldier nodded. North's runaway mine foreman and Lewis' secretary — well, if there were any consolation at all it was that they were both out in the open.

Maung shuffled his feet uncertainly. 'The girl had a typed note signed by Captain Paya. It said she was to be allowed to enter the tunnel to look for a wallet Mr. Lewis had left behind. I — I let them in. They took only about fifteen minutes, then they came out again. She said she had found the wallet.'

'Was she carrying any package when she entered? Or was the man?' Paya's voice was harsh with restrained fury.

'No, sir.'

'A few chemical time fuses and their pockets filled with explosives,' said Cord. 'The rest wouldn't take long. But how did she get this pass?'

'Yesterday I signed the report she typed — and the copies.' Paya wiped a hand across his brow with exasperation at the thought. 'The rest would be a simple forging. But why, Cord. Where does she fit in?'

'She's Nam Ree's daughter,' said Cord quietly. At any other time the look which came on Paya's face would have amused him. But not now. The time for laughter was past, long past.

* * *

Cord and Paya arrived back at the Thamaung camp just as Henry Lewis drove off to carry out his own survey of the damage. He passed them with a curt nod, his face as gray and hard as the granite he'd striven to conquer.

They let him go; they had work of their own to do. But first, Marian Frey was waiting. Cord told her of the tunnel episode and she bit her lip.

'Most of Lona's clothes are still here,' she said. 'But there's a few things missing from her room, enough to fill an overnight bag.'

'She won't be back for the rest of them,' said Cord. He swung off and left her, wanting to be on his own, to feel free to curse himself for the way he'd allowed events to roll on without hindrance.

He and Paya were busy enough for the next half-hour — and ended with nothing to show for it. First there was an interview session with Myi Teri, under guard at his hut. They met a blank, stubborn refusal to cooperate, despite the worst of the soldier's threats. Then they went through a series of questionings with the villagers, project personnel, and outpost guards in an abortive attempt to find some trace of either Nam Ree, his daughter, or her twisted-toothed companion.

Cord was glad of the chance to call a halt when Henry Lewis came back down from the Ridge and beckoned them into his office.

'It could be worse,' declared the U.N. project chief, settling down in his chair with a heavy sigh. 'There's a fortnight's work at least up there, just clearing away the fall and reinstating the tunnel entrance. Even at that, I'm gambling that the real damage is confined to a fairly short stretch and that what lies behind is intact. The time element will be the real problem.'

And time, Cord knew, was the prize Nam Ree sought above all. He nodded, and glanced toward Paya, who sat saddle-style on a chair opposite.

'Well, my course is clear,' growled the soldier. 'More men, more equipment, and then we toothcomb these hills.'

'It wouldn't work,' said Cord quietly. 'The first troop convoy coming over the mountain road would have half a cliff blown down on it. And, remember, the rivers start rising in a couple of weeks. As of now there's nothing anyone can do to stop Lake Mawtayn from overflowing. You'll be virtually cut off once the Sihrong floods, and then Nam Ree can call the tune.'

'All this because the man wants to keep his people in the Thamaung *ching*.' Lewis stared blindly at his desk, hands clasped knuckle-white in front of him.

'I think there is more involved, and that Cord knows it,' said Paya with grim resignation. 'This is a rebellion or the beginning of one. The real moves will be carried out once the river rises, as he says.'

'Then — but why didn't the man wait? Why lose his chance of surprise?' Lewis was bewildered.

'He couldn't,' said Cord. 'He admitted things were getting out of control. When he decided to release you from the tunnel he was both getting himself out of a nasty situation and taking the decision that the tunnel would have to be blown.'

'Well, we can be ready,' declared Paya stubbornly. 'Even if the road was blocked, we could make a landing strip for aircraft. We could hold a perimeter around the dam, then once the Sihrong dried out . . . '

'Would you like to start a war, Captain?' queried Cord. 'Because it wouldn't be hard. The way to the east will still be open. Supposing Nam Ree managed to hold most of a Thamaung 'state' for a spell, long enough to get himself recognized by Peking? They're probably ready and waiting for that right now, and supposing he could whistle up a couple of Red Chinese volunteer brigades any time he wanted?'

Paya cursed slowly and fluently. 'Aid

for a newborn People's Democracy, the old familiar pattern!' He slammed his fist on the desk.

'And still as good as ever,' said Cord bitterly. 'Do you want to know the only people in the world today who can do pretty well what they want? The weakest little pockets of humanity, the fellows who can sit in the middle and play off their big brother neighbors one against the other. Nam Ree may be balancing himself on a knife edge, but if he can keep his nerve he might bring it off.'

He stopped as he heard a knock on the office door. It came again, and Lewis rose, crossed over, and looked out. 'Well, Marian?' The project chief mustered a nod of greeting.

The brunette swept past him. 'Talos, you asked Anna Prinetti to contact you if she remembered anything more . . . '

'Has she?'

The girl frowned, her gray eyes uncertain. 'She says she's not sure if it matters. But she wants to see you.'

'All right.' He rose, looked at Paya, and grimaced. 'Whatever it is, it can't make things any worse.'

* * *

Anna Prinetti was in Marian's room. As Cord came in, she rose nervously, clutching hard at the strap of a small leather handbag.

'Maybe I'm making a fool of myself,' the project foreman's wife began.

He shook his head. 'No matter what it is, it could help.' He waited until Marian had persuaded the woman to sit again. The girl stood behind the older woman, one hand resting encouragingly on her shoulder. 'Like to tell me now?'

She bit her lip. 'It was after you left, after what happened at the tunnel. You asked me about the Pulo shrine, Mr. Cord well — I told you the truth. I wasn't asked to type anything connected with it. But — well — Andy did tell me he'd been there. In fact, he gave me a souvenir from the place for young Victor. He said I was to keep it safely, and that it might bring the baby luck.'

'Can I see it?'

She nodded, opened the handbag clutched on her lap, and handed him a small transparent plastic box lined with white tissue. 'I put it in there for safe-keeping.'

Cord opened the box, then rubbed his chin. All that was in the tissue was a chipping of gray-black stone about the size of a matchbox. 'This was all he gave you?'

'Yes. Andy said — well — I don't know. He seemed to be making a joke and yet to be serious, both at the same time. He said that one day it would be a souvenir people would talk about.'

He looked helplessly across at the girl. She came around, looked at the stone, and rubbed it between finger and thumb. 'Could it mean anything, Talos?'

'It could be just what he said, a souvenir.' Cord frowned down at the chipping. 'Anna, he didn't say anything more?'

'Nothing.' The woman shook her head.

He examined the gray-black chipping

again. 'Still, it's no ordinary piece of granite. Marian, who's the nearest approach to a geologist around here?'

'Dr. Holst, I suppose. He dabbles in it as a hobby.'

'He has books, and he collects little pebbles,' agreed Anna.

'Then I'll find out what he says about this,' decided Cord. 'Marian, better see Anna out. After that, give me a couple of minutes then bring Lewis and Captain Paya over to the medical post.'

Perhaps, after all, they might still have a grip on what Andy Donaldson had tried to say before he died.

* * *

Dr. Holst was snoozing on the dispensary couch when Cord burst in. He sat up with a jerk, a protest blossoming on his lips. 'A man's entitled to his rest . . . '

'Any other time I'd agree,' said Cord sharply. 'But not now. What's this?' He shoved the chipping under the physician's nose.

'Eh?' Dr. Holst scowled and yawned.

'Just a stone — I think.' He took it, rubbed his eyes, and made a closer inspection.

'Well?'

'I don't know.' There was dawning interest in his voice. He crossed to his desk, took out the inevitable bottle, and poured himself a drink. But it lay untouched. 'Where'd you find this?'

'I didn't. Andy Donaldson gave it to the Prinettis as a souvenir for their youngster. He said it came from the Pulo shrine.'

'Did it now?' Holst gnawed his lower lip thoughtfully. 'Andy was in here — oh — less than a week back. Just after his trip. Borrowed a couple of geology textbooks from me; said he was short of reading matter.' He looked at the stone again. 'I can't rush this.'

'You'll have to.'

'Well . . . ' Dr. Holst drained the glass and wiped his mouth. 'I'll try.'

There was a microscope on a bench in the corner. He set it up, used a small hammer and a tiny, diamond-hard chisel to strike a minute flake from the gray-black chipping, and got to work. Every now and again he stopped and swore to himself, while he consulted one or another of a batch of reference books piled on the floor near the bench.

The swearing gradually died. The man was working in absorbed silence when Marian arrived with Lewis and Paya close behind her.

'Well, what's happening?' demanded Lewis as he closed the door.

'Be quiet and wait.' Dr. Holst didn't bother to look up. 'Marian, you can help. There is a little green bottle in the top drawer of my cabinet. Bring it — carefully — that's concentrated sulphuric acid.'

She did as he wanted. The physician lifted his head from the microscope, uncapped the bottle, dipped in a slim glass rod, then let a drop of the acid fall from the rod onto the flake. He waited a moment or two, then put the result back under the microscope, and huddled over it again. This time, when he looked up, there was new excitement in his voice.

'I'll tell you want I think it is, Cord. It has black opaque crystals, some of them twinned — and the chemical reaction tallies. It's a stuff called columbite. If it did come from around here, then plenty of people are going to want to know more about it.'

'Columbite . . . ' Marian was trying hard to remember where she'd heard of the mineral before.

'It's valuable,' said Cord softly. 'Refined, it gives a metal with a very high melting point. It's vital stuff for jet engines and rockets.'

'Very valuable,' agreed Holst. 'Worth — well — maybe any amount, if you need it badly enough.'

'You mean this — this columbite is scarce, hard to find?' questioned Paya.

'Scarce?' The physician gave a hoot of relish. 'I have shares in one of the biggest of the West African mining groups. Their output last year was just over four thousand tons of concentrate tin — and less than three hundred tons of columbite. That's where you usually find it, near tin deposits or' — he stopped, awe creeping into his voice — 'or as compact masses in granite formations! If this is part of a real lode of the stuff, then every last inch of these hills will be put under a fine tooth comb survey!'

'But that was done,' objected Marian. 'The Ronul company carried out a full survey less than three years back.'

'Then somebody was either a fool, a knave, or out of luck,' grunted Dr. Holst, unimpressed. 'Rubies? Rubies are for people, girl. This is the stuff that matters. This is the stuff for nations.'

Talos Cord looked toward Paya. 'I think it means two visits,' he said slowly. 'One to Maurice North, to see if he has a copy of that survey report, and the other to the Pulo shrine.'

'You think this is why Donaldson was killed?' asked Lewis tensely. 'To keep this quiet?'

'It makes the perfect answer.' Cord nodded. 'But the more important question is whether Nam Ree knows about it.'

Captain Paya gave him an odd look. 'That interests me, too, Mr. Cord. *Kaung ba-byi* — I think we should find out together, and quickly. That means going to Maurice North. What about the cave shrine?'

'I could do that,' Lewis volunteered. 'I could take Prinetti with me.'

'And a few of Paya's men for company,' Cord qualified. 'You might run into anything up there.'

The project chief straightened his shoulders, a new spirit in his voice. 'We've been fighting shadows long enough; if there's trouble, at least it'll be trouble we can understand.'

Behind them, Dr. Holst gave a grunt and poured himself another drink. 'I'll have the bandages ready,' he promised gloomily.

* * *

Paya had things to do, including sending off a hastily coded signal to Myitkyina. While the squat, burly soldier bustled around, Cord went through to Lona Marsh's office, ruminated beside her typewriter for a moment, then took one of the sheets of used carbon paper from the tray beside it. He folded the sheet and put it carefully into an envelope.

His next stop was at the guest hut. He opened his suitcase and took out a small black metal box which lay in the bottom right-hand corner. Inside was a Swiss Neuhausen automatic. He fed the gun a clip of fat, glistening 9 mm. Parabellum cartridges, took two more spare clips, and put them into his hip pocket.

Marian Frey was standing just behind him when he turned. 'Talos.' She took a step nearer. 'Maurice can't know. I'm sure he can't.'

He shrugged. 'We'll have to find that out.'

She didn't move, and he could read the anxiety in her eyes.

'Worried about him?' He turned it into a clumsy joke. 'Remember, you're the girl who's not in the market.'

'I'll remember.' She forced a smile, turned quickly toward the door, then stopped again. 'But things can change.'

She had gone before he could think of a reply.

Minutes later he was sitting beside Paya in the driver's cab of the command truck, heading up the valley road.

7

It was late afternoon when the command truck reached the mine at Ronul. Captain Paya's escort of half-a-dozen men stood by their vehicle while he followed Cord up the clattering iron stairway to Maurice North's bungalow-cum-office. The one-armed mine manager met them at the open doorway with a strange mixture of surprise and anticipation.

'Any trouble getting through?' he asked, waving them on into the house.

'No.' Cord shook his head at the question as they were guided into the front room. 'Why?'

'Because I was turned back,' said North with a frown, coming in last of all and standing in front of the empty fireplace. 'It happened only a couple of hours ago.'

'Hmm. We saw no one.' Paya glanced around the room with sharp, unconcealed interest. 'Mr. North, should we take it you know what happened to the

Thamaung tunnel?'

'Unless they're deaf or dead everyone in the valley knows by now,' grunted North sardonically. 'One of my boys arrived with the news just before noon. I got the truck out right away, and half-a-mile down the road we found a quartet of Nam Ree's men waiting. They were friendly enough, but they more or less told me the nearer I stayed to home the better.'

'So you obeyed?' asked Paya mildly.

'My driver didn't stay long enough to let me argue.' North shrugged. 'With a shotgun pointing at his head, I couldn't blame him.' There was a British service Webley pistol lying on his desk. He saw Cord glance at it and nodded. 'I'm not in the mood for taking chances.'

'Even with friends?' Cord's mouth formed a perfunctory half-smile.

'With Nam Ree himself I wouldn't worry. But some of his supporters seem to be getting glory-road ideas.' North shook his head. 'A late apology isn't much use when you've got a bullet in your guts.'

Paya stirred impatiently. 'I would leave the philosophizing for another time, Mr. North. Your company had a geological survey carried out in this district . . . '

'Just over two years ago, yes.' North scratched his head. 'Look, what's that got to do with this load of trouble?'

'It could give us a motive,' said Cord crisply. 'You've got a copy of the survey?'

North nodded.

'Like to show it to us?'

'Like to give me a reason first?' parried the mine manager.

'If you want,' agreed Cord. 'Lona and your foreman blew up the Thamaung tunnel.' He crossed the room and looked out of the open window at the derelict yard below. 'We think Lona killed Donaldson, and we know she's Nam Ree's daughter. Heard enough?'

'Lona is Nam Ree's . . . ' North swallowed hard. 'The idea's crazy.'

'Nam Ree doesn't think so,' Cord assured him. 'He told me himself this morning, just before the tunnel went up. Marsh was her mother's name.'

North rubbed his jaw, still trying to

get used to the idea. 'I knew he was a widower and had a daughter somewhere, but I never knew his wife had been a European.'

'That isn't what matters now,' snapped Paya. 'We need the survey detail, and quickly.'

'I'll get it.' Still shaking his head, North took a fat bunch of keys from his pocket and crossed to an old-fashioned roll-fronted desk. He unlocked it, let the roll-front clatter down, and began dredging through one of the middle drawers. At last he brought out a slim folder bound with blue tape. 'This is a carbon copy; the original went to the company office in London.'

'Thanks.' Cord untied the tape, Paya at his side. Inside the folder nestled a wad of typewritten papers and a collection of sketch maps. At the top was what he'd hoped for, a summary of findings.

'Mind telling me what you're looking for?' North tried to edge between them, a note of growing exasperation in his voice.

'In a minute.' Cord read through the

list of headings, glanced at Paya, then turned back to the summary. Behind them, North lit a cigarette and waited in impatient silence. At last Cord looked up, his face expressionless. 'What do you know about the firm who carried out this survey?'

North removed the cigarette from his mouth and knocked off an inch of gathered ash. 'They're based at Myitkyina. They're small but efficient, and they got the job because their price was right.'

'It would be.' Cord carefully returned the papers to their folder. 'You felt satisfied when they'd finished?'

'They did a thorough enough job,' protested North. 'Their surveyor spent months working on it.'

'But he held out one fact,' said Cord wearily. 'I know. You were only interested in potential ruby strikes. But this report goes into full strata detail, minerals, the lot — with one exception. Ever heard of columbite?'

'Of course.'

'We know there is a deposit of

columbite in the valley,' said Paya bluntly, flicking the report with one stubby forefinger. 'One outcrop is at the Pulo shrine. You didn't know?'

'I don't seem to know very much.' The mine manager bit his lip. 'You're sure?'

'Sure enough for Lewis and Prinetti to be on their way there now,' Cord told him. 'North, why isn't it in this survey?'

The Englishman flushed. 'How the hell should I know? Maybe the surveyor didn't come across it. Maybe there's just a freak pocket . . . '

'Or maybe your surveyor deliberately held it out of his report, but made sure certain other people were told,' growled Paya, slumping into one of the big leather armchairs. 'Are you prepared to swear you knew nothing of this, Mr. North?'

'I certainly am.' North tossed his cigarette stub out of the open window. 'Damn it, if I'd known there was columbite around . . . Look, my company would have been in on the ground floor. We'd have made money, big money.'

'That part makes sense,' agreed Cord.

'But what about the rest? What about Nam Ree. Suppose this is the reason why he's been determined to keep the Pulos here and stop the valley from being flooded. If it is — well — can you blame an outsider if he finds it strange that one of Nam Ree's best friends didn't know about it?'

'Now look, Cord . . . ' The man stopped and his lips closed tight. He paced the length of the room and back. 'I can guess what this is building up to, but you're wrong.'

'Am I?' Cord played him on, knowing he had to achieve maximum effect. 'Suppose again — this time that the original cave in at your mine was a deliberate act because it had hit the columbite vein, the vein that had to be kept secret.' He saw the dark anger gathering in the mine manager's eyes. 'All right, I'm prepared to believe you didn't know. But what about Lona? She was to have typed a report from Donaldson, a report which would say he'd found columbite up at the Pulo shrine. There's solid foundation for what I've said. And if Lona knew, wouldn't it make sense to believe Nam Ree would be in on it, too?'

Maurice North stood silent for a long moment, his eyes on the survey folder. When at last he looked up, the anger had gone and was replaced with something close to pain.

'We lost five men in that roof fall, Cord. Something else collapsed along with it — my personal future.' He gave a brief, bitter laugh. 'Oh, I get a nice chunk of cash from the company out of the compensation the U.N. fund is forking out. Enough to let me make some kind of a new start. But what I wanted was here.' He pursed his lips. 'Well, that's my worry, not yours. And it doesn't alter the fact that the only way I'll believe Nam Ree knew about the columbite is if I hear him say so.'

'That's exactly what we've got in mind,' murmured Cord happily. 'Captain Paya and I want you to take us to him so we can ask just that. Did he know, or, if he didn't, why not?'

'I can send a message . . . '

Cord shook his head firmly. 'No messages. You can take us, and we'll arrive out of the blue.'

'Which will be the best way,' agreed Paya from the depths of his chair. 'Being taken by you should be sufficient safe conduct for us. Mr. North, I strongly advise you to give us this assistance. Otherwise my government might feel tempted to act against a man who has openly admitted giving shelter and comfort to a wanted rebel.'

'That doesn't particularly worry me,' snapped North. 'But if I take you up into the hills, then you'll know the route to take again — and the next time, Captain, there could be a couple of companies of infantry behind you.'

The soldier sat with his head cupped heavily in his hands, his thick lips pouting thoughtfully. 'I am not so naïve as to simply offer you my word. But surely there are ways? A man can be blindfolded . . . '

'And still scramble over the hills?' North gave a grim snort at the idea. 'You'd break your neck — and probably mine, too.' He considered for a moment, then gave a crooked smile. 'Yes, there is a way. But I'll take you on my terms, and with no guarantee that Nam Ree won't decide you've seen too much to be let loose again.'

Paya nodded. 'I agree.'

'What about you, Cord?' demanded the mine manager. 'Remember, I'm giving no guarantees. You're letting yourself in for this of your own free will.'

'I get paid for sticking my neck out,' said Cord with a smile which wisped over the scar on his cheek.

'Right.' North reached out and picked up the Webley, hefting its weight in his hand. 'Remember, I'll have this, and until we get there I give the orders.' He looked at them each in turn, making sure he was understood. Then a new, almost friendly expression crossed his face, and he put the heavy pistol down again. 'Before we do anything, let's eat. It may be quite a spell before we have another chance. Afterward, you'll have to get rid of that escort. Sending them up the valley road would be the best idea.

It could draw most of the attention away from here, and I've a feeling half the battle in reaching Nam Ree will be to get past his men.'

* * *

In a little while the old Pulo housekeeper shuffled in with a pot of strong, hot tea and a platter containing a vast mound of thick-cut sandwiches. When they'd finished the makeshift meal, North left for a few moments and reappeared with the Webley holstered at his waist and wearing a pair of heavy ankle-high boots. He glanced at Paya's footwear and nodded approval, but shook his head over Cord's lightweight brogues.

'You'll have trouble with those. Like me to find you something stronger?'

Cord thanked him, and he went off again to return with another pair of boots. They were a close enough fit to be comfortable.

Paya's task came next, and North insisted that they all go to the command truck. He listened while the burly soldier instructed the escort n.c.o. to make a patrol tour up the valley and then return to base.

'Satisfied?' asked Cord, as the chocolate-brown shape of the truck, aerial swaying above it, growled off a moment later.

'So far.' North waited until the truck was out of sight, then jerked his head toward the hillside. 'Let's go.'

'Now?' Cord blinked.

'Right now.' North gave a prescient chuckle. 'We're going through forest for most of the way. By the time we're finished — well — maybe you'll still be able to get your bearings, but it won't be easy. That way, too, there's a lot less chance of bumping into company.' He turned on his heel and set off.

Cord shrugged at Paya and they began to follow.

Within ten minutes they were deep into the trees and were finding it difficult to keep up with North's long, deceptively smooth strides. Above and around them tall silver fir and laurel towered close and regular, only here and there interrupted by the ubiquitous cherry and broad-leafed magnolias. The thick overhead foliage filtered the sunlight down to a dull, oppressive gloom, and their feet sank into soft fern and moss, the occasional dead branch cracking underfoot like a pistol shot. Insects throbbed around, from thin, vibrant shapes to a fat, clumsy flying beetle with kangaroo-like legs.

The ex-forestry officer kept on, leading them in a twisting, winding route, moving with rhythmic ease, as sure and confident of his way as if he were following a compass bearing. Part of the time they were moving gradually uphill. Cord's chest became a dull ache of pain and the strapping around his ribs soon felt like bands of iron. He could hear Paya panting behind him, as they slogged across one particularly steep slope and reached a stretch of bare sun-dappled rock where the trees fell back.

North stopped short, and they waited while a mottled green shape slid off the rock and moved lazily into the heavy scrub beyond. 'Python,' he said in matter-of-fact fashion. 'They like the heat — sleep out on the rocks. They're all right when they're sleepy.'

Farther on they flushed a small deer. But the main life of the forest was overhead, a twittering, multi-colored chorus of bird life. The greatest gatherings were around the big, pink, tea-kettle blossoms of the magnolia, where the birds scooped and gobbled with their long, curved needle-shaped beaks. The whole riot of color was made more fantastic by the gentle rain of cast-off petals drifting down around their heads.

After an hour North let them rest for a full, blessed ten minutes. Then they were off again, repeating the pattern. But at the end of the third hour they at last broke from the forest belt.

Talos Cord looked around him, gasping for breath, barely able to stand, but filled with wonderment as he looked around. They were high all right, high on the northeast slopes of the Dolpha Ridge, looking out over a landscape of untamed beauty. The mountains beyond seemed clear and startling, wearing their snowcaps like giant ornaments of beaten silver. The valley itself held a blue haze over its forest stretches, and its floor far below them was a green carpet of rich perfection. Cord had a moment of poignant, almost jealous understanding of why a man like Nam Ree — or North, for that matter — should be loath to leave this place, even without the knowledge of the gray-black mineral lying beneath the tranquility.

'How much farther?' Paya was leaning back against a rock, openly exhausted, looking up at the jagged peaks of the Ridge towering above them, his face wet with perspiration.

'Only another mile.' North contemplated his companions with dry amusement. 'We can rest here for a spell. The next stretch is too open to try in full daylight.'

They stayed there while the sun sank lower on the Ridge and the shadows lengthened. Then, as the first hint of lilac dusk tinged the sky, North set them moving. They journeyed in straight-line style, over a mixture of rock and moss and scrub, heading downhill again into the fold between two shoulders of the hills.

North stopped them again near one gnarled, ground-hugging clump of thorn. He seemed to be waiting for something, watching the darkening sky and the rocks below. They heard the sound first — a faint, high-pitched squeaking, oddly muffled. Then, like a puffing smoke cloud, a swarm of specks began rising as if out of the very ground. They circled for a moment before spreading and scattering, the squeaking growing as their wings rustled overhead. The Cave of Bats had been well-named.

'Let's go.' North jerked his head and they moved forward.

A score of paces further on, they rounded another patch of bush — and came face to face with four Pulos. Each of the hill-men had an antique but well-oiled rifle, and each rifle was trained unwaveringly at them.

'We've arrived,' said North.

As advice, Cord felt it barely necessary.

* * *

The rest of the distance to the Cave of Bats, a scant thousand yards, was a march at rifle point. Even after North had argued with the quartet, they were still prodded firmly along the way. The mouth of the *ku* — this particular mouth, Cord corrected himself, remembering the Pulo leader's description of the labyrinth of natural caverns and galleries — was a wide triangular hole in the rock, shielded in part by a tangle of thick-rooted rhododendron. Two more men, each with a leather cartridge bandolier slung over his homespun jacket, one cradling a machine-gun, the other a modern pump-action shotgun, stepped out to meet their escort.

'We wait here,' said North with an uneasy frown after a new discussion had ended. 'They're sending a man in. But I don't like it, Cord; at least one of the quartet who picked us up knows me, knows me well. Yet . . . ' He shook his head.

'You're in bad company, that's all,'

said Cord easily, more easily than he felt. 'What about these two? They don't look like locals.'

'They're not,' muttered North. 'They're southerners by their tongue and build. That's another thing I don't understand.'

The chosen messenger disappeared into the cave and minutes passed while the short, swift dusk began to merge into purple twilight. When at last the man returned, a thin, familiar figure was at his side. Tan Das inspected the visitors, his lips pulling back in a shark-like grin.

'It was not wise to come here, Mr. North,' he said with a sleek swagger. It made Cord glad to note the swollen eye and split lip which were souvenirs of the man's meeting with Prinetti.

'Hello, Tan.' North gave a slow, cold nod. 'They wanted to see Nam Ree and I thought it important enough to get them here.'

'Perhaps you take too much on yourself.' Tan Das didn't trouble to hide the sneer in his voice. '*Ho'ba* — we have both Captain Paya and Mr. Cord . . . '

'We'd have brought your pal Prinetti along, too, but he was busy,' said Cord with lazy insolence which stung the splay-toothed renegade.

Tan Das snarled, then his eyes flicked to Paya's holstered revolver and his rage boiled over. Their guards took a brief, high-pitched tongue-lashing, and even before it was finished, the visitors were being roughly searched and their weapons seized.

'Now things are as they should be.' The ex-foreman looked them over arrogantly.

'And so perhaps we will see Nam Ree,' said Captain Paya with acid dignity. 'I did not come here to be manhandled by underlings.'

Tan Das took a quick half-step and hit the soldier a cuffing backhand blow across the mouth. A *dah* knife held by one of the guards pushed Paya back further against the rock. Tan Das raised his hand again, in almost leisurely style, but before the blow could be struck, a sharp command snapped out from the cave mouth.

Nam Ree came toward them on quick,

cat-like feet, his dress once more the homespun uniform worn by his men. He flashed a look of quick, questioning distaste toward his subordinate.

'I have been questioning them,' began Tan Das in a brisk, confident style.

'I saw your last question,' said the Pulo leader sharply. He brushed the man aside. 'Maurice, I'm sorry.'

'I wasn't the one he hit.' North shrugged.

Nam Ree gave a short, apologetic nod, which took in both Paya and Cord, then swung around on Tan Das. '*Ba pyittha-le?* Why did word they were here not come straight to me?'

'I thought I should find out first why they had come . . . '

The brown, button-nosed face froze into hard, cold disapproval. 'I prefer to conduct my own inquiries on such things, both now and in the future. You understand?' He waited for an answer, a squat, stocky figure with an air of determination.

Tan Das stood silent for a moment, his mouth a thin, slashed line. Then his eyes lowered and he nodded.

'Good.' The Pulo leader was satisfied. He turned back toward North. 'Well, my friend? This is an awkward time to have to greet you and — and you are in even more awkward company.'

'They didn't come direct,' said North, taking the offered handclasp. 'I brought them through the forest.'

'Ah!' Nam Ree chuckled at the picture. 'I thought they looked a little tired. I should have realized you would make it difficult for them to locate this place. Not impossible, but difficult — and as things are, that is enough.' He growled an order to his men and they began to head back to their posts. Only Tan Das remained, his small, quick eyes watching every move. Nam Ree frowned at him. 'You have finished the task I gave you?'

'No, not yet.' The ex-foreman shrugged and went back into the cave on his own.

'Nice company,' said Cord.

'He has his uses — and his shortcomings,' said Nam Ree abruptly. 'Well, shall we go to a more comfortable place?'

They followed him into the cave. Compared with the narrow gallery Cord had sampled, this part of the Cave of Bats was a revelation. The way they traveled was large and wide, lit by oil lamps at regular intervals. After a short distance it branched in two directions. The left-hand gallery was narrow, dark, and uninviting; but to the right the string of lamps continued.

Nam Ree guestured briefly to the left. 'That part we leave to our landlords, the bats.'

The right-hand gallery, in contrast, ran in an almost straight line for about a hundred yards, then developed into a speleologist's paradise of interlinked chambers varying in size from little bigger than a closet to one high-ceilinged cavern the size of a small drill hall. Several of the chambers were occupied, and here and there a face watched with interest as they passed. One branch-off chamber was in near darkness, and inside it several men lay sleeping on straw and blankets. Some chambers were storerooms for food, oil drums, and water; they passed another where pots steamed over a cooking stove.

'You find this interesting?' Nam Ree glanced almost roguishly toward Paya. 'When I was a *ka-ley* boy I explored these caves, miles of them. This is part of the lower level; even today there are still galleries unexplored.'

'It's a — a useful place,' the soldier admitted, stifling a scowl.

'And we could be far away within a very short time,' declared Nam Ree, his deep voice booming and echoing along the natural corridor. 'Outside of my people, few men have seen this place.' He guided them on a little way further, then stopped at one entrance which was covered by a hanging blanket. 'My headquarters, for the moment . . .'

He drew back the blanket and they entered a small cavern, brightly lit by a hissing pressure lamp. Its main furnishings were a selection of old wooden boxes and a map hung from a peg driven into the rock. There was also a folding camp bed in one corner with its blankets folded neatly in army style.

'Find yourselves seats,' Nam Ree invited them. 'And we must wash some of the travel dust from your throats.'

The inevitable *zu* wine and some tin cups appeared from one of the boxes, and the bottle gurgled out a full measure for each of them. Then Nam Ree paused quizzically, cup in hand. 'It is difficult to think of a suitable toast, except, perhaps, to the future.' He chuckled at their lack of reaction and sipped from his cup. 'Now to business. You have come here with some offer?'

'Offer?' Paya blinked at the word.

'To negotiate,' said Nam Ree patiently. 'With the tunnel gone . . . '

'Your daughter and Tan Das did a good job.' Cord nodded. 'But the damage isn't permanent.'

'It wasn't intended to be.'

Maurice North shook his head. 'Look, Nam, let's stop hedging around and get down to why I brought them here. Did you know there is columbite in the valley?'

Nam Ree frowned at them. 'Columbite? I have heard of the mineral, but . . . '

'It's quite an asset,' said North shortly. 'It gives a rare and valuable industrial metal.'

'Then this is good news, very good news!' The man's surprise was either genuine or he was a consummate actor. 'It will bring what we need — a measure of prosperity to bolster independence.'

Paya gave an angry snort. 'This independence nonsense is a pipedream, nothing more.'

'We can make it come true, Captain,' Nam Ree assured him soberly. 'The exact extent of freedom we should have — well — that is something I might be willing to discuss. But there are men throughout the hills ready to take up arms if necessary to achieve what we require.'

'I'm still interested in the columbite,' murmured Cord. 'I'm surprised you didn't know about it; your daughter could have told you.'

The Pulo leader's face darkened. 'Mr. Cord, I have warned you before — Lona has always acted only at my express wish. You are in a difficult position at this moment, here uninvited — where my decision is final.'

'Is it?' Cord shrugged. 'I wouldn't go along with that as far as Lona is concerned. I'd say there's plenty she hasn't told you.'

'Go on, please . . . ' They turned. Lona Marsh stood behind them at the entrance to the chamber, a benignly feminine smile crinkling the corners of her beautifully shaped mouth. She had abandoned the silk and nylon of her usual garb for a more practical outfit of slacks and short-sleeved shirt in a matching bottle green. She repeated her invitation again, as if to an erring child. 'What do you want to tell about me, Mr. Cord?'

'All right.' Cord met and challenged her level gaze. 'You knew there was a columbite deposit in the valley, but you kept it secret from your father. Yesterday you killed Donaldson to stop him reporting the deposit, killed him after using Anna Prinetti to create an alibi for yourself.' He ignored the rumble of anger from Nam Ree. 'Try explaining this away.' He brought out the small envelope he'd prepared at the camp and extracted its single sheet of black carbon paper. 'Like a good secretary, you made a top copy and carbon of Donaldson's memo. He'd expect it. Then, when he was going to sign them, you stabbed him; if the bayonet hadn't been handy you'd probably have had something else in mind.'

'I typed nothing . . . '

He cut her short. 'You destroyed the memo and its copy, Lona. But there was still the carbon paper in your desk, every word clear. You forgot about it, didn't you?'

'It was . . . ' She stopped, her face hardening as she realized how close she'd come to being trapped.

'Destroyed?' Cord nodded, crumpled the sheet of carbon, and tossed it aside. 'You try questioning her, Nam Ree — father to daughter. See how far it gets you.'

The Pulo leader bit his lip, then beckoned her nearer. 'Lona, the truth — did you kill this man?'

She forced a smile. 'Of course not.'

'Then you would not object to having your fingerprints taken,' said Paya suddenly. 'We will find no prints on the bayonet, of that I am sure. But a forensic expert will be at Thamaung today. He will check through the man's room — on his desk, for instance.'

Cord pressed in again. 'Where did you work before you came here, Lona?'

'In Myitkyina.' Her eyes were angry now, the words almost spitting from her lips.

'In a survey office?'

The girl stood silent, but Nam Ree looked at her, then gave a slow, reluctant nod.

'The same firm that ran the full-scale survey for the Ronul company?' Cord didn't wait for an answer. 'The firm that didn't mention the columbite deposit in its report? Do you expect your father still really to believe that it was just chance you managed to turn up later in Thamaung as Lewis' secretary?'

Nam Ree stared at him, his mouth half-opened, his usual all-embracing confidence fading, its place taken by an almost suffering doubt.

'Father . . . '

'Be quiet,' he snapped. 'Maurice, is this true about the survey?'

North nodded. 'It's true. And I'm wondering how much of a coincidence it was that Tan Das appeared at the Ronul mine just before Lona arrived at the project camp.'

'Did you know that Tan Das kept a midget radio transmitter down at Ronul?' chipped in Cord.

'I guessed there would be such a thing,' the Pulo leader admitted. 'He came to me about a year ago and — and told me he had certain friends in the east willing to help if needed.' He rose from his seat and gripped his daughter by the arm. 'Is the rest true?' The grip tightened; he ignored her gasp of pain. 'Did you do these things?'

She looked past him and a glint of triumph chased the pain from her face. 'Supposing it is, Father, what can you do?'

They followed her gaze and saw the

reason for her change.

'He can do nothing, nothing at all,' said Tan Das, leaning against the cave wall almost negligently, as he stood near the entrance blanket, North's Webley pistol in his hand. 'Let her go.'

Nam Ree loosened his grip and the girl stood back, rubbing her arm where the finger marks showed against the skin.

'We've got all the answers we need now,' said Cord softly.

'And it is time my father learned some common sense,' snapped the girl. 'Of course I killed Donaldson. I disliked it, but once he told me what he'd found, it was necessary. He only knew it was a strange mineral. But his report to Lewis would have been enough — and the columbite is needed, vitally needed.'

'By Peking?'

'By Peking,' she snapped back. 'Why else would we bother about a piddling little *taung* bandit and his dream republic of rocks and poverty?'

North stood up, sighed, and shook his head. 'I don't want to be involved in this.'

'But you are involved,' said Tan Das with a quick, wolfish grin at the mine manager's crumpled bearing.

North turned away, as if resigning from the situation.

Nam Ree glared toward the ex-foreman. 'How much do you think you can do alone, you *kwey* — even with my daughter? Put away the gun before I have it taken from you.'

'Nobody will do that,' Tan Das told him. 'The boot is quite firmly on the other foot at the moment, and that is how it will stay. Think of this. You have had several recruits lately, men from the hills, but not men of this valley.'

'Your men?' asked Paya sharply.

'More or less,' agreed Tan Das, pleased at being the center of attention. 'At the moment by,' he grinned, 'by arrangement, there is not a single Pulo in the caves. They are out along the valley, watching roads, scouting, or just waiting to be told what to do.'

Too late to either help or stop him, Cord saw Maurice North make his move. Ignored and forgotten, the mine manager had been edging along the cavern wall, the cup of *zu* still in his hand. Now he sprang, simultaneously throwing the rice wine at his ex-foreman's face. The spirit stung and blinded the man. He clawed at his eyes with his free hand, while the gun waved uncertainly.

But North didn't reach him. At the same moment another gun spoke from behind the blanket curtain. North jerked upright, then crumpled and slumped to the floor. While the shot still echoed, the curtain was torn back and two men in homespun uniform pushed in, each holding a carbine, each watching and waiting for an excuse to fire again.

Tan Das wiped his watering eyes clear of the last of the *zu* and, still blinking, looked down at North and prodded him with one foot. The mine manager groaned, and he turned away.

Cord ignored the threat posed by the carbines and bent over North. He'd been shot high in the chest, a little below the left collarbone, serious enough but not a killing wound — provided he received attention. Cord rose again, taking his time, giving no sign of the hot fury within him.

'You asked about the Pulos, Captain Paya,' Lona reminded him with a sweet, almost girlish smile, acting as if the man on the floor didn't exist. 'All that has to be done is for them to be told that my father is ill, a sudden fever; they know me as his daughter; they will accept my orders as his.' She turned to Nam Ree. 'But it needn't happen like that, Father. You can still lead your freedom fight . . . '

'On what terms?' asked the Pulo rebel gratingly. 'To what end?'

She shrugged. 'On our terms. The Thamaung district will fight for independence, but will need help. That part is all arranged. When it is over — well — all that is involved will be an adjustment of boundaries. Thamaung will be a small protected state within the Chinese People's Republic. You, Father? Well, you can choose. You can be the hero of the valley or you can be its first martyr, shot by' — her dark eyes roamed toward Paya — 'by an army officer who came to you pretending he wanted to arrange a peace.'

Nam Ree stared at her, horror and disbelief struggling within him. He looked at Cord and Paya as if yearning for one of them to tell him this was a nightmare, that sooner or later he'd wake up. But they said nothing, and he clenched his fists, agony in his voice. 'You are my *thami*, my daughter; and yet you could do this, do this to me and to your own people?'

'There are things greater than personal relationships,' she said quickly, avoiding his gaze.

'And more important,' grunted Tan Das. 'Lona, your father will need a little time to consider. Cord, you and the soldier pick this one up,' he prodded North again with his foot.

They obeyed under the menace of the carbine muzzles, supporting North awkwardly between them. North moaned once, then was silent, his face white, his eyes narrow slits of pain. Nam Ree was shoved ahead of them. They were hustled out of the chamber, back into the main gallery and deeper into its length. They stopped just short of the point where the oil lamps ended. A crude wooden door was jammed into a side chamber, secured by a bar across the outside and with a large peephole set in its surface. One of the guards removed the wooden bar and pulled open the door. Nam Ree was first to be pushed into the darkness beyond, then Cord and Paya were prodded after him with their burden.

'In theory, Captain, you rank as the first prisoner of war of this incident,' mused Tan Das with cold amusement as he stood in the doorway. 'Mr. Cord's position is more obscure, particularly as the Chinese People's Republic is not a member of the United Nations. However, we will worry about that later.' He disappeared for a moment, returned with one of the oil lamps, and set it down on the floor. 'We can leave them now, Lona.'

She nodded. 'Father, there will be a

guard outside. It would be foolish to attempt to be a hero in this place. Think over what I have said.'

The door slammed shut, the bar grated into place outside, and they were alone.

8

'I've been in worse places, but not many.' For the tenth time Talos Cord inspected their prison and knew despair.

They'd been half an hour in the tiny, naturally formed cell, its roof sloping sharply toward the floor at one side. The same two guards were posted outside, one or the other occasionally peering in through the slot in the door. The rock chamber was bare of fittings, apart from the oil lamp, whose guttering wick already filled the air with evil-smelling smoke.

But at least Maurice North, resting on a makeshift pillow of jackets, showed no sign of internal bleeding. One handkerchief plugged the neat entry wound in his chest, another stopped the ragged, larger hole where the bullet had reemerged high on his back. Paya had contributed the handkerchiefs, both immaculately clean, and a long strip of cotton cloth from

Nam Ree's turban supplied the bandage that held them in place.

'I had that door fitted myself,' sighed Nam Ree. He was sitting on the floor, his face rueful. 'At the time it seemed a good idea, but I did not expect to be sampling it like this. *Ma kaung* — it is bad. All of this is bad.'

'Didn't it worry you before?' Cord sighed and was more explicit. 'Didn't you have doubts about the way things were shaping up?'

'A few. But none concerning Lona.' The Pulo leader sucked at his lips. 'When she appeared at Thamaung as Lewis' secretary I was happy; it seemed wonderful fortune. She told me she was using her mother's name to avoid embarrassment — and it was the first time I had seen her for many years. A wanted man has little chance of family life. And then, when she encouraged me in my hopes for the valley,' he shrugged, 'if I was blind, all I can say is that she is my only child. Her mother died at her birth.'

'A man can easily be blind to his

child's faults,' said Paya with a gruff attempt at kindness.

Nam Ree nodded. 'Even if you had not come here today I would have had to find out sooner or later.' He still sucked at his lips, seeking for words to explain. 'I met her mother during the war — that last time I was wounded, Maurice.'

'I remember,' said North with an effort. 'The Jap convoy ambush. We didn't know about the escort.'

Nam Ree smiled a little at the far-off memory. 'She was a nurse at the base hospital. They didn't quite like it, but they gave us a wedding present. Later, when I was left with Lona to bring up, I — well — I made arrangements — foster parents. It seemed best, and I always kept in touch. But not closely enough. I knew nothing of how her mind had been shaped.'

'How did you find out she was at the project camp?' asked Cord.

'She sent a message. It was simple enough.'

He didn't press the man further.

Time crept past. Once, the door

opened and they were herded into a corner while one of the guards cautiously exchanged a new lamp for the old. Later, a ghara jug of water and half-a-dozen lengths of thick bamboo were dumped on the floor beside it, then the door quickly closed and was barred once more.

'At least we are to be fed,' grunted Paya.

Nam Ree nodded and, side by side, the two men squatted down to unstopper the bamboo lengths. Inside each was a mixture of rice and vegetables.

'It is cooked like this, in the bamboo,' said Nam Ree in explanation. 'Afterward it keeps hot, as in a Thermos. Maurice, you would like some?'

The mine manager raised himself up a little on his rough cushions. 'No, but I could use a drink of that water.'

Cord gave him his fill, holding the heavy ghara steady at his lips. Then they coaxed North to eat a mouthful of the rice. As he finished, he shivered. 'It's damned cold in this place.'

Cord looked at the others in the dim lamplight. It was cold all right, but Maurice North's skin was almost burning to the touch.

The second time the door opened, it was to admit Lona. Flanked by the two guards, she stood looking at them for a moment. Her face remained expressionless. 'I thought I would say good night, Father,' she said finally. 'Unless, of course, you would rather leave these others and have a more comfortable night. You've only to say. I am still your *thami*.'

'There are some things I can't help.' Nam Ree looked very deliberately away from her. 'What I want for the valley is not just a change of overlords.'

'But it wouldn't be like that,' she urged him with sudden intensity. 'All domestic matters would be left to you . . . '

'Would your friend Tan Das say that, too?' asked Cord mildly from his corner. 'Or should I call him Comrade Das?'

'His correct title is colonel,' said the girl brusquely. She saw the surprise on Paya's face. 'He outranks you, Captain.'

'In which army does he hold this commission?' demanded the soldier stiffly.

'The Burmese Peoples' Volunteer Brigade . . . '

Paya snorted. 'That rabble! A handful of camp-followers at the heels of the Chinese.'

She ignored the insult. 'And North, how is he?'

'Still able to answer for himself,' said North, forcing out the words. 'Lona, when are you going to wake up to the fact that the party's over? Your father won't play. Without him, you can't have your little uprising. Anyway, there's two weeks to go before the rivers raise Lake Mawtayn enough to flood the Sihrong, and by that time the whole Thamaung district could be brought to its knees.'

She nodded. 'I hope so. Because tomorrow we send out word that the time has come. The Pulos will rise and seize the valley.'

'What?' There was stark horror in Nam Ree's voice. He lurched toward her, then stopped as one of the guards swung his gun suggestively. 'Don't you understand what that means? The government knows now about the columbite, Lona. They'll rush in men and equipment. Our people may have a few days of triumph, but then — then it will be a slaughter.'

'Perhaps.' She shrugged, unimpressed. 'But the result will be the same — a cry from the oppressed, a persecuted minority who have seized independence.'

'Then your people can move in from the east to answer this 'cry,' grab what they want, and next thing call a halt saying they'll agree to a cease fire under U.N. control.' Cord stared at her, fascinated by the cold-blooded butchery which the plan encompassed and the calm, factual way in which the full, feminine figure before him could treat it. 'Ever seen people killed in a war, Lona?'

'I have already killed in my war,' she said simply. 'We have worked hard and long for all of this, Mr. Cord. It would have been easy, perhaps, just to send arms across to the Pulos, but it would have made things too — too apparent.' The girl pursed her lips. 'Anyway, Mr. Cord, what business, what right have you to meddle in all of this?'

'Everybody seems to get around to asking that,' agreed Cord softly. 'Perhaps I just don't like trouble, regardless of who causes it. People matter to me, not flags or politics.'

She looked at him for another long moment, then shrugged and glanced toward Nam Ree. 'If you change your mind, Father, tell the guards. They know what to do.'

Nam Ree had his face turned away from her, away from the light. He didn't move.

She waited, then her mouth tightened and she turned on her heel and left. The guards followed, the door slammed shut, and the bar grated back into place.

'There goes a she-devil if ever I met one.' Cord whistled. Then he winced. 'Sorry, Nam Ree.'

Slowly the man turned his face toward them. The tears on his cheeks glistened in the lamplight. 'Why be sorry, Mr. Cord?' He asked. 'Who can complain at truth?' He gave a long, sighing breath. 'All I know is that I had a dream and now it has become a nightmare.'

'It does tomorrow,' said Cord heavily, 'unless you can do something about it.'

'You mean' — a spark of hope lit up the Pulo leader's eyes — 'you mean I should agree to help them, then seize my chance?'

'You wouldn't get that chance,' said Cord definitely. 'The first wrong note out of you and you'd disappear from view.'

Paya clasped his hands together, flexing his strong broad fingers until the knuckles cracked. 'If we could get out of here, if I could get my hands on a rifle . . . '

'Then we'd all be happy,' agreed Cord with a cynical grin. 'Why don't you ask the guard to let us out?'

The soldier scowled. Then, slowly, his expression altered. 'We can't. But Nam Ree can.' His voice dropped to a murmur. 'The men outside have their orders. If we made sure they had a chance to obey them, and if they had to rescue Nam Ree from our anger . . . '

The Pulo leader gazed at him, struggling to understand. Then he gave a low, rumbling chuckle. 'Captain, I have misjudged you.'

'It could work,' mused Cord. 'Especially if we left it until early morning, when they're less likely to be on their toes. But what happens when we get outside? If we have to get out the way we came in, we wouldn't have a chance. We'd be setting ourselves up like targets in a shooting gallery. How many men do you think Tan Das can rely on?'

'Perhaps twenty, no more than thirty in this place.' Nam Ree shook his head. 'I should have realized what was happening — these strangers he brought to me in twos and threes.'

'That's past,' said Cord quietly. 'What time should the guards change?'

'If they remain on the routine I set up, at six A.M.'

'Right. Supposing Paya's idea worked and we got out of here. Is there another way to the outside?'

'Yes. A little deeper into the caves you come to — to almost a maze of small chambers and galleries. One gallery leads to the west. Halfway along its length there is a fork. The left fork is just broad enough, and no more, for a man to climb. It comes out on the west side of the Dolpha Ridge, just above Lake Mawtayn.'

'And the other?' asked Paya grimly.

'Follow that and you are finished,' said Nam Ree in an earnest whisper. 'It goes deep and narrow, so narrow that a man can barely crawl at places. It comes to a dead end.'

'Under the lake?' Cord spoke loudly in sudden interest. He cursed to himself, but when no sound came from outside, no face appeared at the peephole in the door, he asked again in a hoarse whisper, 'Do you mean the other gallery runs under Lake Mawtayn?'

'As far as I can guess,' agreed Nam Ree. 'When the lake is high and the Sihrong is flooding, then there is one place in the gallery where water drops from the roof. I have seen it happen when I was much younger.'

'Supposing we got out of here,' urged Cord. 'There must be only a shelf of rock between the gallery and the lake. Don't you see what that could mean?'

'If we had explosives, yes,' grunted

Paya with little enthusiasm. 'A little work, and your Thamaung project would have no need of a tunnel.'

'There are enough explosives not far from here,' said Nam Ree, his voice strangely strained. 'Explosives and grenades — they are stored in another part of the caves.'

'Could we reach them?'

'Yes. There is usually a guard, but,' the Pulo seemed reluctant to go on.

'But if we did it . . . ' Cord had a new realization of what he'd been asking. Blow a hole in the bottom of Lake Mawtayn and the pressure of water bursting through the Cave of Bats as a result would have all the power and force of a hydraulic ram. Anything — anybody in its path would be swept along like dirt before a hose jet. He swallowed. 'She's your daughter . . . '

Nam Ree looked at him steadily. 'I think we should decide when this will begin, Mr. Cord.'

* * *

They waited until five A.M. by Cord's watch. Two hours had passed since the guards had last looked in to change the flickering lamp for another, and Paya, looking out through the peep-hole in the door, reported that the two men were sitting drowsily side by side a few feet along the gallery.

Their preparations were made, their parts rehearsed as far as possible. Nam Ree, his jacket once again over his shoulders, walked quietly to the door, then glanced back at Cord. Like the others, he moved in his stocking feet.

'Right,' murmured Cord.

Nam Ree beat a quick tattoo with his knuckles on the door, then gave a quiet call. Outside, one of the guards looked up, rose, and began walking over to their cell. Next moment, Cord and Paya had pulled Nam Ree roughly away from the peep-hole — and the man outside looked in on what seemed a desperate free-for-all on the floor of the rock chamber, all three men grunting and growling like animals, as they fought and rolled around.

The wooden bar was pulled free, the

door swung open, and Cord took a sudden, hefty blow on his shoulder from a rifle butt, as the guards broke up the struggle. Paya was similarly shoved clear, and Nam Ree rose shakily to his feet, muttering quickly to his rescuers. They nodded and one of them found time to grin as Paya growled a searing curse. Then they beckoned Nam Ree to move out ahead of them, their attention fixed on the two battered, angry men who still seemed ready to swoop back on their prey.

Nam Ree took a step behind them, and another. The first of Tan Das's men began to turn to follow him, and the Pulo brought his right hand from under his jacket in a lightning-swift move. The baton-length of bamboo clenched in his fist smashed a savage, clubbing blow against the man's temple. The thud was heavy and solid; the bamboo was packed tight with chips and flakes of rock prized from the walls of the cell. While the man was still falling, even as the second guard's mouth began to open to shout an alarm and his rifle swung up, the bamboo club hit again, this time in a swift, vicious upstroke. It took the guard on the jaw with a crack of breaking bone.

Cord caught the man's rifle before it had time to hit the ground. Nam Ree clung to the bamboo for a moment, then helped himself to the first guard's *dah*. The rifle he left for Paya. Cord hesitated, then helped himself to the other man's *dah* — a beautifully balanced length of dull, razor-honed metal.

Softly Paya went out and took a few steps along the lamplit gallery. 'So far, no alarm,' he murmured, 'but we should leave quickly.'

'Strange company, Captain,' murmured Nam Ree.

Paya grinned and checked the rifle, clucking his tongue in disgust at finding the breech empty. He jacked a shell into position and signified his readiness.

They bound and gagged the two unconscious guards, using the men's belts and strips of their tough homespun clothing. When they left, the cell door closed behind them, it was once again

Cord and the soldier who helped North along, while Nam Ree led the way, heading into the darkness with the shielded lamp casting the faintest possible glow ahead of them. They were still in their stocking feet, moving silently, the rough surface of the rock jabbing through the thin protection, coarser fragments biting and cutting a growing number of tiny lacerations in the skin. But the weapons in their hands made for confidence, and the grim purpose ahead filled their mood with a sharpened determination. Even North caught the spirit, struggling to keep moving with tight-lipped courage.

Cord was surprised at just how soon they made their first stop. Nam Ree shined the dull pencil of light to one side, showing a narrow, burrow-like hole going off to their right.

'This part I can do alone,' murmured the Pulo, as they lowered North down to the floor to rest. 'It should not take long.' He left them the lamp and, the *dah* in his hand, wriggled into the hole before they could stop him. Minutes passed, but at last they heard a faint scuffling and he reappeared.

'There was a sentry,' he told them softly, his face like an ancient bronze sculpture in the dim glow. 'But Tan Das is careless. I would always have two men, each to keep the other awake.' He moved into the glow of the lamp and Cord saw the dark staining on the *dah's* heavy blade.

'The sentry?'

'He will not trouble us,' said Nam Ree soberly.

They left the two rifles beside North and followed the Pulo back along the narrow burrow-like tunnel. It ran for close onto forty feet and ended with a drop down into a chamber about the size of a double garage. Cord came last, after the two Burmese, sparing only a grim glance toward the lifeless figure sprawled a little to one side. The *dah's* blade had taken the man on the crown of the head, splitting it open like a chopped orange. The same glance gave Cord the lay of their surroundings. They had entered at the rear of the cavern. Its main entrance, a broad, dimly-lit passageway, lay just beyond the body.

Nam Ree gestured toward the crated stores piled around the walls. 'We want two green boxes; they contain plastic explosive. There is also a black metal box, like a small suitcase; it holds grenades.'

They found all three items without much effort. Cord used the blunt tip of his *dah* as a jimmy to lever open the first green box and gently unwrapped one of the greaseproof paper-covered slabs within. The soft brown substance dented like putty as he pressed his thumb against it. Plastic explosive was just that — press it, squeeze it, drop it, and nothing would happen. It would burn fiercely but harmlessly; it could be molded to any shape; but add a simple cap detonator, and a parcel no bigger than a man's lunch box could obliterate a house.

Cord closed the box, checked the second container, and looked up. 'What about a fuse and detonators?'

Nam Ree frowned. 'I can only find this. We had to use the rest for the Thamaung tunnel explosion.' He held a single clockwork time fuse, the fifteen-minute type, with its own built-in chemical detonator.

'It'll do.' Cord helped him carry the box of grenades over to their escape burrow, then waited until the Pulo had squeezed himself in and had backed out of sight, dragging the box with him. A moment later Paya brought over the first box of plastic explosive, laid it down below the burrow, and went back for the second box.

What warned Cord, he couldn't be sure. But he turned in time to see the open-mouthed guard standing at the cavern's entrance and the pistol swinging up in the man's hand. Then Paya had catapulted himself across the distance, arms out-stretched, grabbing for the intruder's throat. The pistol's bark was little more than a muffled cough, firing with its muzzle jammed against the soldier's body. As Paya toppled back, while the guard was still frantically pushing the suddenly limp, still encumbering form aside, Cord came in. The *dah* in his hand sang a slicing arc, and the shudder of the metal as it hit bone jarred through his arm. The heavy blade took the guard between shoulder and neck, cutting deep. He died with no more than a violent, sobbing grunt, and Cord laid down the *dah*, sick at the butcher work he'd done.

But there was Paya to be taken care of. Cord knelt beside the soldier, rolled him gently over, and felt for the man's pulse. Paya groaned at the movement and his eyes blinked open.

'How do you feel?' asked Cord, knowing the ridiculous inadequacy of the words.

Paya grunted, moving his muscles with exploratory caution, and winced at the result. '*Ma thi-bu* — as if I have been kicked by a bullock.'

Cord parted the front of the man's powder-scorched combat jacket, looked, then gave an incredulous grunt. The bullet had hit the broad brass buckle of the army webbing belt beneath — the metal showed a clear, broad dent where the slug had flattened. Paya's shirt was torn, and blood was already soaking through from a shallow, harmless surface graze. Cord unbuttoned the shirt, explored along the raking wound, and found the twisted, barely recognizable bullet lying just under Paya's left armpit.

The soldier's mouth fell open when he saw the bullet. 'So I cannot even be properly wounded . . . '

'Don't sound so disappointed.' Cord listened for a moment. The pistol shot, though muffled, would still have carried through the echoing galleries. But their luck seemed to hold, either that or Tan Das's men slept soundly. Cord saw the automatic lying where it had fallen from the guard's hand, picked it up, and recognized it as his own — the Swiss Neuhausen taken from him when they'd arrived. A closer look at the man he'd killed, and he remembered the face from that time on.

A rustle to the rear brought him spinning around, the Neuhausen at the ready. But he relaxed as Nam Ree's head cautiously appeared from the burrow hole and the Pulo jumped down beside them.

'A second guard' — Nam Ree took in the scene and gave a brief understanding nod — 'it seems Tan Das did not forget.' He looked toward Paya. 'Can you move without help?'

'Of course,' growled the soldier unconvincingly, pulling himself to his feet with their help and doubling up again for a moment with the muscular agony that resulted. 'At least — in a moment.'

Cord glanced at his watch. It was fifteen minutes after five; the guards were due to be changed in something like forty-five minutes. 'Can you make it back through the burrow on your own?'

Paya straightened up a little and nodded agreement. They let him go through first, then followed, each dragging one of the boxes of plastic explosive. Nam Ree had another, equally valuable find — an electric flashlight he'd suddenly remembered was kept among the crated stores. When they reached the other end of the narrow tunnel they found Paya leaning against the wall beside Maurice North. The soldier was obviously determined to keep going without help, equally obviously little able to do more than drag himself along.

'Gives you quite a problem, doesn't it?' queried North wryly. 'Three boxes to carry, only two of you able to do it, and me to lug along just to complicate things.'

'We'll manage.' Cord turned to Nam Ree. 'How far to where the gallery forks?'

'Four, five hundred yards, not much more.'

'Then let's get started.' Cord shoved the automatic into his pocket. 'This is how we'll do it, North. Nam Ree and I'll take this stuff along to the cave fork. You and Paya will stay here until we come back. If anything happens — well — Paya can use one of the rifles.'

They left them there and set off, Nam Ree carrying the heavy grenade box under one arm as if it were a parcel of groceries and using the flashlight with his free hand. Cord came close behind, one box of the lighter plastic explosive under each arm and gritting his teeth at the way in which their weight seemed to increase. The pain in his chest was back again, like a constant, nagging toothache which grew worse with each successive step.

For ten long minutes they moved along the gallery, but it was slow progress, often crawling on hands and knees at frequent stretches where the roof narrowed down, pushing and pulling the boxes along with them until they could stand more or less upright again. Cord was on the brink of being forced to call for a respite when he heard the Pulo give a satisfied growl. They'd arrived at the fork.

He laid down his burdens with a sigh. Nam Ree nudged him and silently pointed the flashlight upward and to the left. The left-hand fork was a long, almost straight shaft, narrow, steep, and barely the width of a man. But when Nam Ree flicked out the beam for a moment, Cord could see a small gray circle of dawn light clearly visible above.

Going back the way they had come, but without their loads, was a very much easier affair, and close to the halfway mark they came across their companions. Paya was staggering along, the oil lamp in his left hand, a rifle slung over that shoulder, and his other arm supporting North. The soldier's face was beaded in sweat and he was close to collapse, as they took over the mine manager's weight. They let the two men rest until their breathing steadied a little, then helped them both along to the fork and their first sight of the promised safety above.

'We'll get you up first,' began Cord.

Still panting for breath, Paya shook his head. 'A good soldier always protects his line of retreat,' he gasped. 'We will wait here. You two finish what has to be done.'

'North?' Cord looked at the mine manager. But North's head was hanging limp and he was barely conscious due to sheer exhaustion.

'We should go,' agreed Nam Ree.

The right-hand fork led to a narrow, snaking path which soon became little more than a crack running through the rock, so confined that there were lengths where they had to scrape through on their stomachs, pushing the boxes ahead of them. Once Cord felt a sudden dampness beneath him, heard the slow drip of water from the roof above, then felt the drops landing on his body as he passed. A stifling, claustrophobic fear of the unknown began creeping over him, and he lost count of the number of times he banged his head or had to force his shoulders through narrow bottlenecks, all the time wondering if this nightmare would ever end.

When it did, and he could glance at his watch, he was surprised. It had taken them barely twelve minutes. They were in a small funnel-shaped depression with room enough to lie opposite each other and place the boxes between them. There was even a foot or so of roof space above their heads. Cord opened the plastic explosives boxes, packed the grenades from the third box around them, then took one of the slabs of explosive and fashioned it into a crude cup. In the middle he inserted the fifteen-minute-clockwork fuse and detonator.

'Ready?'

Nam Ree nodded. Cord waited until the Pulo had wriggled around and was ready to leave, then tapped him on the shoulder. As the man set off, Cord triggered the clockwork and stayed only long enough to hear it ticking before he followed him.

The grim knowledge of what was to happen sent them back at a furious pace. They reached the end of the fork in a panting eight minutes and found Paya equally tense and anxious. North sat beside him in the darkness, clear-eyed again and husbanding his strength for the next ordeal.

The climb to the surface was simple and, for North, mercifully swift. Paya went first, followed by Cord, who half-dragged North up after him, while Nam Ree came last, also helping the pathetically weak mine manager along.

When at last they squeezed out onto rough, tufted grass on an open hillside they sank down, mutually exhausted, gulping in the clean mountain air, savoring every lungful.

At last Cord raised his head. Lake Mawtayn lay at the foot of a short, gentle slope below them, a silver-gray sheet of placid water in the early morning light. Reeds grew around its shallows and a big, solitary kingfisher majestically stalked his breakfast along its fringe.

'How long?' asked Paya, a rumpled, dirt-smeared figure, his clothing ripped and torn, a dried streak of blood from a rock graze lacing across his forehead.

Cord looked at his watch. 'Two minutes.'

Slowly Nam Ree stood up and looked down at the hole through which they had come. Cord turned away, leaving the man to his thoughts, taking the chance to move Maurice North into a more comfortable position.

The two minutes passed, then another two. Cord lit a cigarette, and Paya seemed about to say something, but then shook his head and remained silent.

After five minutes Cord accepted the fact that the clockwork fuse had failed — and knew what he had to do. Down below them, very soon, the guards would begin changing, and their escape would be discovered. The missing explosives would give Tan Das an immediate clue.

Cord beckoned Nam Ree closer. 'Does Lona know about the gallery under the lake?'

The Pulo leader chewed at his lip thoughtfully. 'I can't be certain, but, yes, I think I told her once.' His eyes widened as Cord took a first step toward the hole, and he gripped him by the arm. '*Ma ne* — this is my task, Mr. Cord.'

'Not the way I see it,' said Cord quietly.

'No? I told you I have lost my dream.' The Pulo looked at him with deep, sad eyes. 'When a man is without a cause and has lost his hopes, he has little left to live for. I think you know something of what I mean, Mr. Cord. More than once I have had a glimpse of sadness, almost a longing, in your face, and have wondered why.'

'It's too long a story.' Cord gently removed the hand gripping his arm. 'I think I can make it there and back.'

'Without a time fuse?'

'I've an idea about that,' Cord told him. 'Look, man, you've done enough, and whatever else she is, Lona is your daughter. Anyway, I may need help getting back out. That's where you come in. You can take that rifle down to the gallery fork and wait. You heard what Paya said before — a good soldier always guards his retreat.'

Nam Ree was undecided for a moment, then gave a slow nod. 'I will be there, at the fork.'

Going back alone along the narrow underground fissure with the flashlight beam cutting a lane into the darkness ahead was somehow less of an ordeal than Cord had imagined it would be. The worst places, where he had to squeeze a way through, were almost old friends, and the patch of damp rocks with its water drips from above constituted a welcome landmark — even though the flashlight beam was showing the first signs of losing its brilliance, a warning that the battery's life was fading.

Once he'd reached the end of the long, lonely crawl and was beside the explosives again Cord propped the flashlight against the boxes and set to work. The clockwork fuse had jammed with, ironically, less than a minute of its life remaining. He discarded it and picked up two of the grenades. One went into his pocket, the other he placed beside the flashlight. Then he pulled off the torn, bloodstained remnant of one of his socks and carefully unraveled a long length of its nylon thread, testing every few inches, knotting the strands tightly together whenever a break occurred. Next he took the book of matches from his pocket. He removed one match, placed it to one side, then bound the open book to the grenade with the matches face out and turn after turn of thread pulled as tightly and as close to the match heads as possible.

He sat back for a moment, then, gently, feeling his heart thumping, an uncertain prayer on his lips, he pulled the release pin from the grenade. The threads took the strain of the firing ratchet's spring, and he had to wait again, forcing the trembling from his hands, before he could go on. Another short length of nylon thread was used to bind one of his last cigarettes to the grenade, so that one cigarette tip was against the match heads and the other protruded free.

He was ready with a makeshift fuse which should last, with luck, the time he needed. Cord picked up the single match he'd laid aside, struck it carefully on the rock, held the grenade against his lips, and lit the protruding end of the cigarette. He took two firm, steady drags to make sure the cigarette glowed to life. Then he extinguished the match, laid the grenade down in the nest of plastic explosive, and started back.

If he had moved quickly before, his pace was now break-neck. He clawed his way over the rock floor, ignoring the sharp contacts his head and body made against roof and ridges, refusing to allow anything to slow him — all the time urged on by the thought of that glowing cigarette gradually burning down, down to the book of matches, the flash of flame that would follow, the instant burning of the nylon threads, the release of the grenade ratchet with its five-second fuse.

Near disaster came when his head

banged against one unexpected overhang of rock. The flashlight fell from his hands, but stayed intact, still giving its feeble yellow glow. He shook the whirling haze of pain from his head, brushed the trickling blood from his forehead, and started off again, just as an echoing bedlam of gunfire came from the cavern ahead. The chatter of an automatic weapon joined in the row, and a bright burst of light suddenly blossomed like a gaudy flower in the black darkness before fading down to a steady glow. As the light steadied, there was a further burst of gunfire.

Cord moved on, but more slowly. The fork junction which led to safety was just ahead, but as he drew nearer, his pace reduced to a cautious crawl, he saw that the light came from a burning pool of oil lying only a matter of a few yards down the main gallery below the fork. How it had been done was self-explanatory — a smashed kerosene lamp lay in the middle of the burning pool. Even as he watched, a rifle spat from the exit shaft and was answered by half-a-dozen booming shots from the far side of the glowing light.

Tan Das and his men had arrived, and Cord was well and truly trapped. He inched nearer the junction, just into the fringe of the reflected light, and promptly regretted it. He heard an excited shout, then a renewed burst of fire, and the scream of ricocheting bullets seemed all around as he propelled himself back.

The situation could hardly be worse. Nam Ree from his post at the escape shaft could hold his opponents at a distance for the moment. But he couldn't provide the covering fire Cord knew he'd need if he were to reach the exit shaft alive. Yet if he stayed where he was . . .

A vague shape moved for a moment just on the far fringe of the reflected glow. Cord jerked the Neuhausen from his pocket and slammed two quick shots at the spot, to be awarded by a cry of pain. But then the automatic rifle hosed a wild answering burst at him, and he hugged the rock floor as the bullets lashed and whined their vicious message. A black object sailed through the air, and a second kerosene lamp crashed into the blazing oil, bursting on impact, its fuel boosting the flames to new brilliance.

There could only be seconds left now. Cord felt the hard bulge of the grenade in his pocket and moistened his lips, knowing that he had to judge it right — everything right. He put the automatic back in his pocket and brought out the grenade, gauging the distances. He had five yards to cover, five yards to the fork and the exit shaft, five yards he could take in a quick hands-and-knees crawl.

Nam Ree's rifle barked again, and was answered by a new sound, the dull, reverberating boom of a double-barreled shot-gun. A hail of lead pellets whipped and scoured the rock.

Cord drew the pin from the grenade and threw the little bomb in an underarm lob, which carried every ounce of strength and hope he possessed. The grenade flew through the air, past the blazing oil and into the darkness beyond. He readied himself, counted the seconds, then the lower tunnel erupted in a vivid white-cored flash and blast. He heard screams, but he was already on his way, propelling himself on all fours, scampering dog-style over the burning oil, feeling its tongued flame scorching his face. He reached the exit shaft and tumbled against Nam Ree's burly shape just as the automatic rifle opened up again.

Next moment a dull, heavy, distant boom beat against his ears. The whole gallery seemed to quiver, then the blast wave swept along like a buffeting gale of wind.

'Up, quickly!' Nam Ree threw his rifle aside and pushed Cord on. The firing had stopped, and whatever fresh sounds there might be were drowned by the rumbling, hissing thrust of a new power, a power which swept the stale air before it like a piston driving through a cylinder. The roar and rush of air increased while they clawed their way up the shaft, and Cord was still yards from the beckoning daylight when a torrent of spray and water howled up the shaft like a jet, swamped over him, then just as quickly sank down again, trying to claw him back with it. He clung to the rock, jammed his shoulders against the roof, his feet against the floor, and struggled on.

Just as quickly as it had begun, it ended. He scrambled on up the rest of the long, upward-angled shaft, Nam Ree miraculously still close behind. Then he had reached daylight and Paya was hauling them both into the open.

Cord stood there, swaying on his feet, looking out at Lake Mawtayn. A hundred yards off shore the placid surface of the water had been transformed. White spray flung itself into the air around the vortex of a whirling, spinning, cone-shaped depression. At the rate of thousands of gallons a second the lake was being sucked down into the Cave of Bats. He thought for a moment of the people down there, of Lona Marsh and Tan Das, of the force like an express train with which that rush of water would hit and smash its way on, taking everything before it.

He turned away and looked at the others. Their eyes, too, were on the whirling vortex — Paya solemnly, almost compassionately grave, Maurice North with a look of weary satisfaction on his pain-lined face, and Nam Ree, standing a little way apart from them, molten grief in his very stance, lips moving in words which no man was to hear.

* * *

The helicopter found them almost an hour later. It hovered, then swept in and touched down with a rush of dust and wind from its noisy, milling blades. Two figures jumped out and came rushing toward them.

Cord surrendered himself to a pumping handshake from the first of their rescuers.

'Would you mind telling me what the hell is going on, Talos?' demanded Karl Steeven. The newly arrived U.N. Field Reconnaisance man — young, lean, and sandy-haired — cloaked his concern behind a freckle-faced grin, as Dr. Holst puffed up the slope to join them. 'I get here expecting to have to bail you out of trouble, then what seems like five minutes later there's a flood pouring into the valley.'

'We didn't have time to send out

invitations,' said Cord, forcing a weary, answering smile.

'That's what I thought.' Steeven nodded. 'Anyway, I grabbed Doc Holst here, shoved him and a couple of the toughest-looking army boys I could find into the chopper that brought me, and we came looking for you.'

'A good thing we did,' grunted Holst, giving Paya a quick nod of greeting and glancing with only momentary curiosity toward Nam Ree. He knelt down beside Maurice North, giving a cluck at the mine manager's pallor. He took North's pulse, touched the bandaged wound gently with his fingertips, and looked around at them. 'The sooner I can move him back to camp and then on to a fully equipped hospital, the better.'

'You mean you're going to do it right away?' asked Steeven.

The physician shook his head. 'I'll do what I can for him here first. Why?'

'I'd like to hop back over the Ridge and into the valley,' said Steeven briskly. 'I think Talos deserves a quick bird's eye view of what's happening. Supposing we fly over, drop down near one of the army patrols, and send the chopper straight back for you?'

Holst glanced toward the helicopter where the two soldiers they'd brought were already unloading a stretcher. He nodded agreement. 'All right, but don't keep me waiting.'

'Let's go then, Talos,' said Steeven. 'I still want to know what's been going on.'

'I'll get around to it.' Cord gave a crooked grin and followed him down the slope.

As soon as they were aboard, the helicopter lifted and, its wide blades churning, swept them in a climbing course up and over the Ridge. Cord had a quick, panoramic impression of the wild hills and the cool, lordly mountains beyond, then Steeven nudged him and pointed down almost straight below.

They were swinging down and into the Thamaung Valley, a valley fast being transformed. Just beyond the nose of the hovering machine Cord saw a vast spouting jet of water cascading out of the lower hillside and rushing down toward the valley floor. The jet sprang from between two almost overlapping shoulders of the Ridge, the main gateway to the Cave of Bats. Here and there along the same stretch of hillside smaller outbursts of water poured in white torrents from among the rocks, marking the location of other, smaller caves which linked with the underground maze. The rushing water was already spreading fast over the valley; the new lake was being born.

The helicopter's engine note changed. Their pilot turned from his controls, shouted something lost in the roar, and the machine swooped lower to hover near the fringe of the flood where the water was no longer a white fury but had settled into a succession of swirling currents. Cord saw some smashed boxes and other debris bobbing and floating, then a body caught between the branches of an uprooted, half-submerged tree. Another body floated face down in the shallows, limbs moving with the pull of the currents. The Cave of Bats had been cleaned, completely and finally.

'What about the villagers?' Cord's voice was heavy and remote.

Steeven shrugged. 'They'll be okay. The army's moving in, evacuating people to higher ground as a first step. No need to worry. They've closed the sluices at the dam so that there'll be no damage to the south. The boys at the dam reckon it'll be a day or two before the valley floor is really covered, and a week or so after that before there's any sizable head of water built up behind the dam. They've plenty of time to get organized.' He pointed down at the swirling flood. 'All your own work?'

Cord nodded. 'More or less,' he said shortly.

His companion recognized the signs and said nothing more.

* * *

The helicopter landed them on high ground on the far side of the valley, close to an army truck unloading a party of Pulo families it had brought out from one of the villages near the Thamaung River. The River was now a raging expanse of water swollen more than a score of times its normal width.

As soon as the two U.N. men were clear, the helicopter rose again, climbing fast and heading back on its mercy run. Steeven led the way over to a fallen tree trunk, waited until Cord had sat down, gave his friend a cigarette, and waited again.

Gradually, as Cord unwound, he told his story. When he had finished, he gave a slow, almost unbelieving shake of his head.

'What happens now?' demanded Steeven.

'Little or nothing.' Cord took a last draw on the cigarette and ground the stub against the tree's moss-covered bark. 'There'll be no rebellion, no excuse for any 'volunteers' to come swarming over. They needed that excuse. Try it any other way and it would amount to open war. But now, with the columbite deposit known and Burma able to pour in men and equipment, Peking will write the whole episode off as a loss.'

'They'd be crazy to do anything more,' agreed Steeven.

Cord nodded, watching the nearby huddle of villagers sorting out the bundled possessions they'd been able to salvage. 'These are the only people who've suffered, and we can make it up to them. Anyway, when the Burmese start mining the columbite from the hills they'll need plenty of labor. One way and another, there's going to be a reasonable helping of prosperity around here. Lewis' team can still drive their tunnel through the Ridge to Lake Mawtayn, then cap off the cave flow.'

'Then it's over.' Steeven eyed him quizzically. 'Over for you, too. Leave any loose ends to us. You can head back to the fleshpots any time you want.' He glanced down at Cord's bare, dusty feet and pursed his lips. 'First, though, I'll see what I can do about those.'

The sandy-haired Field Reconnaisance man strolled over to where the Pulos were beginning to set up camp and returned after a short time carrying a pair of native leather *chi-nin* sandals. 'Try them,' he invited. 'Judging by what I had to pay, I've just made a major contribution to local relief funds.'

The sandals fitted comfortably. A little later, the U.N. men hitched a lift on a truck going back to the project camp, and finally reached the Thamaung compound about noon.

Water was already building up behind the vast concrete curve of the dam, and the project camp bustled with feverish activity. Soldiers were among the work parties busy unloading stores from a newly arrived convoy of trucks, and more soldiers were helping to erect the scattering of temporary brushwood-and-canvas shelters going up on the fringe of Frajon village to help cope with the arriving refugees.

'Busy as bees,' grunted Steeven as they climbed down from their truck. 'Makes me feel almost unemployed.' He saw Cord glancing around, hardly listening, and tapped him on the shoulder. 'Looking for somebody?'

Cord gave up scanning the crowded compound and shook his head.

‘Good, let’s go and see if Doc Holst is still here,’ suggested Steeven.

They found Holst in his office, humming a tune to himself as he stitched a deep cut in a truck driver’s hand. ‘Won’t take a moment,’ he assured them. The deft fingers finished the job, cut the nylon thread, whipped a bandage around the wound, and then he sent the man on his way.

‘Now.’ Dr. Holst looked at Cord, noting the shallow surface cuts and grazes on his hands, the dried blood which still streaked his forehead from the gash on his scalp. The physician sighed, dragged the bottle and a glass from his desk drawer, and filled the glass close to the brim. ‘This is what you need most, Cord. Get it inside you, and I’ll tend to the rest.’

‘We came to ask about North,’ began Cord.

‘Drink it,’ ordered the physician, already setting to work with a gauze pad liberally soaked in antiseptic. He nodded as Cord took a long gulp of the whisky. ‘Don’t worry about North.

The helicopter flew him out of here for Myitkyina. They've got all the facilities if there's any need for surgery, but it shouldn't be necessary. I cleaned up the wound; he's had a blood transfusion; and I pumped in a hefty dose of penicillin. There's not much chance of infection.'

'And Paya?' Cord winced a little as the dabbed liquid cleaned another graze.

'Him?' Dr. Holst gave a barking laugh. 'Going around happy as a dog with two tails, showing everyone that damned belt with the dented buckle. Internal bruising, of course; he'll feel sore for a day or two.' He stopped, holding the gauze pad in mid-air. 'Funny thing happened, though. You remember the native who was with you when we landed?'

Cord nodded and took another long sip from his glass.

'Well,' the physician frowned, 'once I'd fixed North up and made him ready for the helicopter, I found Paya was still there but the other fellow had vanished.'

Cord glanced toward Steeven and saw the faint grin which creased his freckled face. He kept his own expression to one of mild curiosity. 'What did Paya say about him going off?'

Dr. Holst shrugged. 'It didn't seem to bother him. He said the fellow was just a Pulo who'd found you and had helped you out. Any idea who he was?'

Cord shook his head.

'Pity. I thought we might have fixed up some kind of a reward for him.' Holst finished his task by lightly taping the scalp gash, and sat back with a grunt. 'That should do you. If you want to see Paya, he's over at Lewis' office.'

Cord thanked him and left.

Steeven drifted off, heading for the radio truck. Back in New York, Andrew Beck would be waiting for a report; and with two men now on the spot, he'd accept no excuses for being kept waiting.

Cord crossed the compound alone, entered the administration block, and pushed his way into the project chief's office.

Captain Paya was alone in the room, standing studying one of the maps on the walls. He looked around, and a broad beam spread across his face. 'I only heard a minute ago that you had arrived,' he greeted him. 'If it is Henry Lewis you want, he is back in camp; but both he and Prinetti are working over at the dam.'

'I came looking for you,' said Cord, lowering himself into a chair. 'Dr. Holst patched me up a little. He was also telling me about — about the native who got away.'

The soldier gave a friendly scowl. 'Sometimes a man has been hurt enough, Mr. Cord,' he mused. 'I think it can be justice, not mere compassion, to give such a man a fresh start.' He folded his arms, his face serious. 'In my report Nam Ree will be listed as having died in the caves while helping us. He will not be back in this valley. I know Mr. North will agree with my report. Will you?'

Cord nodded. The Pulos could have their martyr now. But more important, Nam Ree would have the chance to get away from the debris of his dreams.

'Good!' The soldier was relieved.

'Ah — and I have a message for you from Miss Frey!'

'Marian . . . ' Cord's voice showed his immediate interest. 'Where is she?'

Paya blinked. 'At Myitkyina by now. I thought Dr. Holst would have told you. She went out in the helicopter with Maurice North.'

'I see.' Cord rubbed one hand across his chin, feeling the coarse stubble of beard. 'Well?'

The soldier frowned, recalling the words. 'She said to tell you that if you followed, the market was waiting. Does it make sense? Of course, there is the bazaar at Myitkyina . . . '

'That's not quite what she had in mind.' Cord grinned. He cheerfully helped himself to one of the cheroots from Lewis' supply and put it in his shirt pocket. 'There's a man wandering around outside, sandy-haired. His name is Steeven. He's taking over from me as of now.'

Paya showed his surprise. 'You are leaving?'

'As soon as I get cleaned up.'

They shook hands.

Cord left, went to the guest hut, treated himself to the luxury of a wash, a shave, and clean clothes, put the Neuhausen back in its box in the suitcase, and was ready.

The Renault pick-up was where he'd left it in the parking lot. He climbed in, laid the suitcase on the passenger seat, lit Lewis' cheroot, and started the engine.

Ahead on the hill road, the cherry trees were at the thrilling peak of blossoming. It would be a hard drive, but Cord could be in Myitkyina by evening.

He rammed the pick-up into gear and sent it bouncing off.

THE END

Other titles in the Linford Mystery Library

A LANCE FOR THE DEVIL
Robert Charles

The funeral service of Pope Paul VI was to be held in the great plaza before St. Peter's Cathedral in Rome, and was to be the scene of the most monstrous mass assassination of political leaders the world had ever known. Only Counter-Terror could prevent it.

IN THAT RICH EARTH
Alan Sewart

How long does it take for a human body to decay until only the bones remain? When Detective Sergeant Harry Chamberlane received news of a body, he raised exactly that question. But whose was the body? Who was to blame for the death and in what circumstances?

MURDER AS USUAL

Hugh Pentecost

A psychotic girl shot and killed Mac Crenshaw, who had come to the New England town with the advance party for Senator Farraday. Private detective David Cotter agreed that the girl was probably just a pawn in a complex game — but who had sent her on the assignment?

THE MARGIN

Ian Stuart

It is rumoured that Walkers Brewery has been selling arms to the South African army, and Graham Lorimer is asked to investigate. He meets the beautiful Shelley van Rynveld, who is dedicated to ending apartheid. When a Walkers employee is killed in a hit-and-run accident, his wife tells Graham that he's been seeing Shelly van Rynveld . . .

TOO LATE FOR THE FUNERAL
Roger Ormerod

Carol Turner, seventeen, and a mystery, is very close to a murder, and she has in her possession a weapon that could prove a number of things. But it is Elsa Mallin who suffers most before the truth of Carol Turner releases her.

NIGHT OF THE FAIR
Jay Baker

The gun was the last of the things for which Harry Judd had fought and now it was in the hands of his worst enemy, aimed at the boy he had tried to help. This was the night in which the past had to be faced again and finally understood.

MR CRUMBLESTONE'S EDEN

Henry Crumblestone was a quiet little man who would never knowingly have harmed another, and it was a dreadful twist of irony that caused him to kill in defence of a dream . . .

PAY-OFF IN SWITZERLAND
Bill Knox

'Hot' British currency was being smuggled to Switzerland to be laundered, hidden in a safari-style convoy heading across Europe. Jonathan Gaunt, external auditor for the Queen's and Lord Treasurer's Remembrancer, went along with the safari, posing as a tourist, to get any lead he could. But sudden death trailed the convoy every kilometer to Lake Geneva.

SALVAGE JOB
Bill Knox

A storm has left the oil tanker S.S. *Craig Michael* stranded and almost blocking the only channel to the bay at Cabo Esco. Sent to investigate, marine insurance inspector Laird discovers that the Portuguese bay is hiding a powder keg of international proportions.

BOMB SCARE — FLIGHT 147
Peter Chambers

Smog delayed Flight 147, and so prevented a bomb exploding in mid-air. Walter Keane found that during the crisis he had been robbed of his jewel bag, and Mark Preston was hired to locate it without involving the police. When a murder was committed, Preston knew the stake had grown.

STAMBOUL INTRIGUE
Robert Charles

Greece and Turkey were on the brink of war, and the conflict could spell the beginning of the end for the Western defence pact of N.A.T.O. When the rumour of a plot to speed this possibility reached Counter-espionage in Whitehall, Simon Larren and Adrian Cleyton were despatched to Turkey . . .

CRACK IN THE SIDEWALK

Basil Copper

After brilliant scientist Professor Hopcroft is knocked down and killed by a car, L.A. private investigator Mike Faraday discovers that his death was murder and that differing groups are engaged in a power struggle for The Zetland Method. As Mike tries to discover what The Zetland Method is, corpses and hair-breadth escapes come thick and fast . . .

DEATH OF A MACHINE

Charles Leader

When Mike M'Call found the mutilated corpse of a marine in an alleyway in Singapore, a thousand-strong marine battalion was hell-bent on revenge for their murdered comrade — and the next target for the tong gang of paid killers appeared to be M'Call himself . . .